PERFECT DRUG

Dark Knights in the City

MELINDA OWENS

Cover design by – Designs by Stacy
Cover art by Stacy Pardu
Editing by Kimberly Dawn
Book interior design by – Deena Rae; E-BookBuilders, adaptation for ebook

For information contact:
Melinda Owens
www.melinda-owens.com
melindaowensauthor@gmail.com

File version: 202111026.006

OTHER BOOKS

The Secrets We Keep

Perfect Drug

Strange Love

Wicked Game

Come Undone

Bittersweet Symphony

CONTENTS

Other Books....c
Dedication....g
Acknowledgements....i
Perfect Drug....k
Chapter One....1
Chapter Two....9
Chapter Three....13
Chapter Four....19
Chapter Five....23
Chapter Six....29
Chapter Seven....37
Chapter Eight....43
Chapter Nine....47
Chapter Ten....53
Chapter Eleven....59
Chapter Twelve....65
Chapter Thirteen....73
Chapter Fourteen....79
Chapter Fifteen....87
Chapter Sixteen....91
Chapter Seventeen....95
Chapter Eighteen....101
Chapter Nineteen....111
Chapter Twenty....115
Chapter Twenty-One....121
Chapter Twenty-Two....125
Chapter Twenty-Three....131

Chapter Twenty-Four 137
Chapter Twenty-Five 143
Chapter Twenty-Six 147
Chapter Twenty-Seven 153
Chapter Twenty-Eight 157
Chapter Twenty-Nine 163
Chapter Thirty 171
Chapter Thirty-One 177
Epilogue 181
Bonus : Strange Love excerpt 187
Chapter One 189
Chapter Two 191
Have you Read these? 195
About Melinda 199

DEDICATION

This entire series is dedicated to my bank family, especially Jessica and Debbie, who understood the dark place I was in when they offered, and I took the job there, and has helped nurse me through it over the past year. They have no idea what they've done for me, and this dedication is a tiny payback for the sanity they have provided me. Thank you guys so much.

ACKNOWLEDGEMENTS

I have to acknowledge my husband, who has stuck by my side no matter how difficult I make that for him to do. He pretends that I'm perfect and there's nothing wrong with me, when it's clear to me, I'm a hot mess.

My editor has been so supportive and amazing, my boss has been the best, and my bestie, Allison has let me sit on her couch with my laptop on several occasions while I whine about website maintenance.

This is my tribe, and I've ever grateful for it.

PERFECT DRUG

Book One of Dark Knights in the City

Charlie Delmonico is a fixer. It's what he does for a living. He fixes all the city's problems.

For a fee.

And he wants to fix Amelia's problems. Or use her for a fix, whichever works best.

Amelia works in the lobby of a building, until Charlie offers her a job she can't refuse. Does she want to be fixed, though? Or does she just want Charlie to see her? To know her?

When Charlie gets involved with a deal involving four other guys, to ruin the city's leader of the underworld, Amelia gets stuck in the middle.

She sees his true colors, and it tears them apart.

Even though Charlie is her perfect drug.

PERFECT DRUG

CHAPTER ONE

Today was the day she was sure she'd lose her job.

Late, again. Amelia tried not to think about it, since there wasn't a damn thing to do to fix things. She'd left as soon as she could, but driving in traffic when you know you're late is so stress-inducing anyway. It was impossible to speed to get there on time, since there was a traffic accident ahead. Everyone else was stuck too. Nothing to be done for it.

This was her third time being late in a month, and she knew she would be in trouble for it. She'd tried talking to Neil, her boss. She'd explained that everyone else was trying to get to work at the same time, and it didn't seem to matter how early or late she left her house, she was still borderline late almost every day. She'd asked for a different schedule. If she had to be there at seven instead of nine, she could leave at six and actually get there on time. There wouldn't be as much traffic.

But he'd told her when she'd applied for, and gotten, the job that started at nine a.m., that's when she needed to be there, period, or he would find someone who could.

The last tax notice had come yesterday, and thankfully, she'd opened it before Gram had. No telling what her great-grandma would have thought about seeing the news. It basically said the county would take hers and Gram's home and sell it if they didn't pay the back taxes in two weeks.

And she didn't have it.

That was one of the things her grandma had taken care of without saying a word. When she'd died, Amelia had suddenly been in charge of everything. Suddenly in charge of her grandma's mother,

Amelia was not excelling at this adulting thing. Ever since she'd left for college, she had made one mistake after another. And now the family home was at stake, and she was stuck in a shitty job she was about to lose.

She inched by the accident that had held up traffic, snorting at the flat tire on the car, not quite out of the road. There were three wreckers, waiting to be called upon, taking up the entire lane. So it wasn't really an accident at all. Just a flat tire taking up valuable highway real estate.

After Amelia passed it, the bottleneck was gone, and she zoomed the rest of the way as fast as she could.

But it wasn't fast enough.

Amelia rushed up the steps to her office building, not having the time to admire the gloomy windows she loved. The architecture was what had initially drawn her to this building; tall, dark windows, spires and gargoyles, it was something out of a novel, and her imagination had captured her months before.

Now it was just a building where she worked. The magic had disappeared from the first interaction with her supervisor, the building manager, Neil Owens.

Lech.

She rushed over to her station at the desk in the lobby, where she greeted employees, visitors, and helped the wayward ones find their destinations.

"Hi," she muttered to the guard, Larry, without looking up. She was focused on not drawing attention to her tardiness, but Brooke noticed.

Of course.

"You're late again," she scoffed as she examined her manicure. "Neil won't like it. He said—"

"I know what he said," Amelia mumbled as she tossed her purse and bag under the desk and sat in her chair to clock in on her monitor. "Gram had an issue this morning, and I had to deal with it."

She'd started making her pickles early today, and Amelia hadn't been prepared for it. After she'd emptied the jars from two days ago, and then the drive…

A massive box of stationary was unceremoniously dropped on the desk in front of her with a loud thud that made her jump in her seat.

"Glad you could join us, Miss Flores." Neil's voice dripped with disdain over her shoulder. "I need these addressed and in the mail by lunch. They're due to go out today. The addresses are in your email."

He stood behind her, too close. Brooke was looking up at him with a grin on her face. Amelia hated them. She was convinced they had something going on. As the building manager, Neil had more power than he deserved. He was in charge of cleaning, security, and maintenance as well as the building employees.

Like Amelia, as he constantly reminded her.

Right now, as close as he was, she could feel the heat of his body on the back of her head, where his crotch was pressing into her ponytail, messing up the curls she had carefully done before she'd realized she'd forgotten to wash Gram's pickle jars.

Nobody else could see it, with the possible exception of Brooke, who was blindly greeting people who entered the building and offering to look up and give directions to where they needed to go.

Meanwhile, Neil's dick was pressed into the back of Amelia's head.

With a sigh, she leaned forward to open her email and start addressing envelopes.

"You know you are on the last straw here, Amelia," Neil had bent to whisper in her ear. "If you don't finish this mail before you take your lunch, you'll be in my office by one." The words uttered in her ear left a slimy promise in their wake. She didn't want to be in his office, ever. She could only imagine the begging and pleading he would want her to do to keep this job.

Suddenly, the air thickened and she knew exactly why. It happened every morning, when *he* came in. She could feel the air move around her, prickling her senses with an awareness. Her eyes rose to find the tall commanding figure standing directly in front of her.

"I'll triple whatever he's paying you to quit right now and come work for me."

Charlie Delmonico.

Against her will, she sighed at the deep voice that brooked zero arguments. As always, she gazed at the plump lips, the chiseled features, perfectly combed light-brown hair, and then moving down to the rock-hard chest and upright shoulders. The man exuded authority in his expensive suits and wool overcoat slung over his arm, briefcase dangling from his hand. She waited for him to turn and continue to the elevators, like he always did, but today something was different.

He was looking at her.

He was standing here. At her desk. In front of her.

Had he spoken to her?

She blinked, realizing yes, he had spoken to her.

What had he said?

One eyebrow raised, he was waiting for an answer, and everything inside her said this man was not used to waiting. For anything. When he spoke again, she couldn't take her eyes off his lips. "I guess I was wrong then?"

He *was* talking to her.

"Neil, I quit." She reached under the desk for her purse and bag, and stood, pushing Neil backward with her chair, since he was in her space.

"You can't just come down here and hire her like this," Neil sputtered.

Mr. Delmonico turned to the security guard manning the desk next to them. "Larry, will you please send the last fifteen minutes of security footage from that camera to my phone." He was pointing to the camera that captured the angle showing Neil grinding his crotch into the back of her head. "Also, if you could find the footage from 10:53 last Wednesday in the banquet kitchens, that would be exceptional."

Neil was protesting. Brooke was gasping, showcasing a pretty pink tongue surrounded by red lipstick that matched her fingernails.

Brooke and Neil had a habit of going off together, and Amelia had suspected something, but their reaction was priceless, and she grinned as she walked around the desk to join her new boss.

"Right then, come on." He led the way to the elevators and joined the small crowd of people waiting. She stood directly behind him, trying not to stare. People around them seemed to take a step away, as if they knew of Charlie Delmonico's power and were afraid of it. They stood there, together, alone, silently.

Hire her? For what? Did she even care at this point?

Every morning, she saw Mr. Delmonico as he entered the building, greeted him, and watched him go to the elevators. The building held all sorts of offices, from oil companies to law firms to sales and service companies. She had no idea what he did, but judging by the private driver that let him off at the curb, dressed in a dark suit every morning, he was successful.

The elevator chimed and the doors opened. Amelia hated these elevators. She hated glass elevators in general, but these in particular since the building was so freaking tall. But triple pay was enough to get on them.

She followed Mr. Delmonico as well as a few others onto the elevator, and as soon as the doors closed, she spun around, not willing to watch the landscaped atrium floor fall out from under her.

This way, she faced the tall, dangerously good-looking man whom she would no longer be looking at from afar as he came in the doors and silently made his way to the elevators.

Of course, he was looking at her. His lips were pursed, as if he were trying to decide what to do with her. It was almost as if she were a bug or something slightly distasteful. Should he squash her with his shoe, or take her outside to let her free? Either way, he was clearly uncomfortable with her.

He apparently thought enough of her to hire her, so something there must appeal to him. Although, he wasn't looking at her that way. She hadn't realized exactly how tall he was, and right now, he looked at her with his head straight and eyelids drooped, down his nose. Literally looking down his nose at her.

With the other people in the elevator, they were closer than she'd ever been to him, and his cologne was intoxicating. It was cool, yet spicy, certainly expensive, and Amelia fought the urge to close her eyes and inhale the masculinity.

Instead, she stared at his neck while the doors opened and closed, letting people off, until they were alone in the elevator.

Amelia's mouth was dry, like Sahara dry. It felt full of sand, her throat gritty. It didn't help that he also seemed to be swallowing more than usual. She could tell because she was staring at his neck.

His neck was tan and smooth, his Adam's apple prominent, moving with each swallow. When she knew they were alone, her eyes moved higher to his. They were dark brown, almost black, and wholly on her. There was an interest in them now, as if the bug was a puzzle and he was trying to figure it out. Amelia swallowed, hard, and licked her bottom lip. Her mouth was so dry. When the elevator dinged a spell was broken, and he stepped back and gestured for her to go first.

His office was the only one on the floor, and she murmured approval as they entered and she saw a massive desk in the first room, with glassed-in offices, expensively furnished. One was a conference room, one a sparsely furnished office, and one obviously his. Large desk, leather chairs, and a laptop and telephone. Another room wasn't glassed in, but the door was open to reveal stacks of file boxes.

She walked to the desk in front, assuming it was hers, and turned to face him.

"Before you begin, there is a nondisclosure agreement. After you sign, I'll give you your contract, detailing your duties and pay scale. You have the rest of the day to review it, let a lawyer look at it, whatever you need to feel comfortable with it. You are under no obligation to sign. If you don't sign it, you can walk out of here right now."

His voice was smooth and held a trace of an accent she couldn't place. Admittedly, she hadn't heard everything, she was so focused on his voice. He could read her a grocery list, and she'd be enchanted.

"Okay," she agreed, and he handed her a piece of paper from his briefcase he'd settled in a chair. She signed it while he hung his coat in his office and got a stack of papers from his desk drawer.

"You didn't read it," he stated as she held the paper out to him.

"I know what NDAs are. I don't talk about anything. There's no one for me to talk to anyway." She shrugged as she spoke, finding his expensive shoes fascinating. They surely cost more than her entire wardrobe. Her skirts and blouses from online discount stores in China couldn't compare.

"Then I'll leave you with the contract. Have it on my desk first thing in the morning." He cleared his throat, nodding once before he strode back into his office and shut the door. The glass windows gave her a clear view of him taking off his suit jacket and settling himself behind his desk. She watched him as he unbuttoned his cufflinks and rolled up his shirt sleeves, the movements sensual and deliberate. Then he opened his laptop and started clicking around, his phone next to it and a small pad of paper.

Focus, Amelia. He's not hiring you to stare at him.

She skimmed the first page, finding it looked pretty standard. She would do simple administrative assistant tasks with other duties as assigned, including some travel. Amelia would take phone calls, make appointments, type, file, and answer emails.

Simple.

When she looked at the pay page, she saw there was an enormous sum of money at the forefront for a work wardrobe, including traveling clothes. It was more money than her house.

She found the blank at the end of the papers and signed them, walking them to Mr. Charlie Delmonico's office.

This was a no-brainer.

CHAPTER TWO

Charlie already had a headache. Between this upcoming trip to the Cayman Islands, and the enchanting waif downstairs—correction, in his front office—he was already busy, and it wasn't even ten thirty.

His phone was ringing, almost as soon as he walked into his office.

"Delmonico." He knew who it was. He'd already had one conversation with Mr. Savage, the guy running against the incumbent for mayor. Charlie didn't have any specific political affiliations. He didn't even vote. It seemed to be bad for business.

"It's me again. You said you would get this done. I need it done. He's kicking my butt in the polls."

Delmonico stifled a sigh. Instead, he watched Amelia as she sat and flipped through the pages of her contract. She pursed her lips beautifully as she read, the pink of her tongue peeking out of the corner of her mouth. "And I will. Do you want to know the plan?"

"No! I don't want to know anything!"

"Then let me do what I do, and you do what you do. Smile for the cameras and claim ignorance when it happens. Don't forget to be apoplectic and express a ton of sorrow." Amelia flipped a page, crossed her delicious legs, and leaned back in her chair. He saw the moment she read the pay scale. Her chest stopped rising and falling with her breaths and she uncrossed her legs and leaned forward. She mentally counted on her fingers and then did it again.

"What are you going to—never mind. I don't want to know anything."

"Goodbye."

Savage was whinier than most, but he would be okay. If he would just trust the process.

Amelia Flores flattened the contract on her desk and ran her palms over it before grabbing a pen and signing it.

He shifted his eyes to his laptop, pretending to reorganize some shipping schedules and open a bank account for a client, when Amelia knocked at his door. Not that she was far from his mind.

Truth be told, he wasn't organizing or opening anything. He was picturing destroying her innocence on a beach in the Cayman Islands.

"Here you go," she said brightly. Too brightly for where his mind was. "Where would you like me to start?"

He pretended confusion. "You didn't have time to read it."

"I read enough." She clasped her hands behind her back, which only served to press her tits out. Like he hadn't noticed them in the loud polka-dotted top she wore. It was one of those retro fifties things, and he supposed it went well with the pencil skirt she wore. But it was too damn tight. He could see a tempting flash of skin between the middle two buttons when she stood like that.

He stood and walked around to the front of his desk, leaning on it and crossing his ankles.

"I'll need you to start by scanning in the files in those boxes." He nodded to the store room. "Then I'll need you to create files that have some semblance of organization on my server for them, and shred the hard copies. After that, I'd like some sort of lounge area. The kitchenette should suffice, but I'll need a coffee pot and fridge and things of that nature. In the meantime, there is a trip to the Cayman Islands next week. We'll be gone six days. You'll need to shop accordingly."

He was making stuff up for her to do. He didn't really need an assistant. Or a lounge, although a decent coffee maker would be nice. The only thing he needed was arm candy, because in his line of work, a single man didn't always get the job done as efficiently as a married one. She'd caught his eye on her first day, her wide doe eyes seeing everything. Her innocence calling to him like a siren every morning when he came in to work.

"You'll have access to my budget," he stated. "And give me your sizes. There are things I'll need to procure for you." He walked back around and sat, making a mental note to call the guy and get her a passport. "That is all."

"I can't take a trip out of the country for six days." Her words were quiet and as he looked at her, she saw her worrying her lip with her teeth.

"You *just* signed the contract. You will take the trip. Make other arrangements for whatever you need to. I need a wife in the Cayman Islands, so we'll be honeymooning. Appearing to honeymoon, of course." Discussion closed, he bowed his head and made a shooing gesture with his hands.

She was *his* now.

"Okay." She sighed. "But what exactly do you do?"

What did he do? There were a lot of names for what he did, none of them very agreeable. It was what he'd been good at his entire life, and instead of rolling over and becoming the peacemaker of whatever social dynamic he was a part of, he'd managed to turn it into a position of power. From foster homes to adult life, he'd procured things for people, solved problems, and managed to make a tidy sum as well as a wealth of networking opportunities. In other words, blackmail when necessary.

"I help people take care of things." He made a quick list on his notepad, then handed her the paper. "Go shop at these places. I know the sales associates. And get some nicer clothes; that blouse is an eyesore."

With a small sigh, she turned and exited his office.

CHAPTER THREE

A few days later, Amelia was getting on well. As well as could be expected anyway. She'd had to change things up with Gram, of course, to make allowances for the new schedule. After shopping the first day and discovering that Charlie Delmonico had a black credit card that worked at all the exclusive boutiques she'd never even been inside before, she'd showed up early to work, and stayed as late as he did, which was late.

It had been weird for her. At the stores he'd listed for her to shop at, the saleswomen seemed to know she was coming, and fortified with her list, they'd piled her arms full of clothes she could never see herself ever wearing. Ball gowns, bathing suits, professional clothing well above the title of administrative assistant, and jeans that cost more than she was making, even at her new salary.

So she owed him to be the best she could be for him. Besides, she'd been admiring him from afar for months. Now she was in the same office as he was and could watch him through his glass walls.

He had a habit of leaning into his hands and ruffling his hair when he was bothered by something. He would roll up his shirt sleeves as soon as he got into the office, and while he sat at his desk and emailed and called people, he would run his hands through his hair and across his face almost constantly. But as soon as he was getting ready to leave his office, or if someone was coming in for an appointment, he had a procedure of rolling down his sleeves, fastening his cufflinks, and combing his hair. As easily as he rumpled himself to work, he straightened himself for display, oozing a put-together confidence she knew she needed to emulate.

And she tried. In the short time she'd been here, she'd made sure her hair and makeup were straight. She'd been sure to have a manicure on the first day, and had kept it neat-looking, even though she couldn't go for the fake red nails that Brooke had. But as little as he looked at her, Charlie still seemed to approve.

She was scanning the files as he'd asked her to. It was pretty tedious work, and she skimmed them out of curiosity as she worked, but she didn't really get anything. Just names and dates. Scant details. She still didn't really understand what he did.

Then one name caught her eye, and she paid closer attention.

Scott Hidalgo. He was the shortstop for the local baseball team. He'd been in the news a few months ago with a stalker who had overdosed and died one night. It had all been very dramatic, the crazy woman dying in a car outside his house.

Scott's name was there with a date. Then a woman's name and a date. She used her phone to google the woman, and yeah, she was the stalker.

Amelia's eyes went to Charlie's office, and she saw him on the phone, looking at his computer screen. He was completely absorbed in his work. She read the article attached to the woman and saw the sensational words describing her death at the hand of too much cocaine.

She was putting two and two together. Charlie Delmonico had told her he solved problems. A stalker would definitely be one of those problems. And he had killed her.

She shook her head. Wow. She was getting a ton of exercise jumping to conclusions.

Amelia let out a snort and continued working. But names kept flashing at her. Names connected to some sort of publicity she could remember. An abusive marriage to a rock star that had been all over the trash magazines last year, but he'd suddenly left her and his career had ended abruptly. A senator's custody battle, another politician rumored of beating his wife, a local TV celebrity who had been stalked by a fan. The list went on and on.

Now, she had a clear understanding of what he actually did for a living and why she was being paid so well. Not that any of this was definitive proof he'd actually done anything. It could just be a hobby of collecting information about gossip around town.

Right. Because Charlie Delmonico seemed like just the sort to be obsessed with celebrity gossip, she thought sarcastically.

She watched him again through the window, his strong forearms and rumpled hair. The lips he pursed as he listened to whoever was on the phone talking. The eyes that were looking at her, dark and dangerous.

Wait. He was looking at her. And she was staring.

She swallowed and looked back at her own computer screen, pressing some buttons to look like she was busy. Amelia needed to stop reading and actually do some work.

That's what he was paying her to do. She wished she hadn't gotten nosy. Amelia should be upset, but he was paying her enough not to be. That didn't make any of this right, and she felt a little bit differently about him now.

He was a killer. And his work didn't look entirely legal.

**

That night, when he came out of his office, her desk was surrounded by boxes. He frowned at them as he left. She'd found more work to do than he'd realized. Maybe he needed to come up with an actual project for her to do. She was likely to learn something in those boxes that she wouldn't like.

He forced himself to focus on the present.

He needed to go visit that punk and get back into the darkness where he was comfortable. Back in his car, Luther nodded in the rearview mirror at him.

"That girl? I like her. She's nice." Luther had started driving Amelia to work after Charlie noticed she drove a beat-to-hell Taurus that had to be twenty years old. She probably wasn't happy about it, but he needed her at work in one piece.

"To Midtown. Drive around slowly," Charlie cut him off before he could continue extolling Amelia's qualities. The punk's name had been Caleb, back when he was useful. Now he ran drugs for Bascom Forrester, who'd been around a while, and he went by the stupid moniker of Desert Eagle. He carried around a brass-plated monstrosity of a gun by the same name. It was too big to hide anywhere, so he kept it in a backpack. Charlie rolled his eyes just thinking about it.

As they drove back into the city, Luther carefully maneuvered the car where Charlie had directed. As he drove up and down the streets of Midtown, Charlie kept his eyes peeled for the kid.

"There. Pull over."

Luther complied, and Charlie rolled down his window, motioning for the kid to come over.

"Get in. Let's go for a drive. I have a proposition for you. One I think you'll like."

Caleb got in, his eyes eager for the fix Charlie promised him, curiosity getting the best of him. Charlie actually liked these brushes with Caleb's element. The stupidity that oozed from Caleb, aka Desert Eagle, served to boost Charlie's confidence, his notion he had chosen the right path in life. The dark nights when he wondered who or what he was, he remembered times like this.

"Who you partying with tonight?"

"I've got a deal with some bigwigs in an hour over at The Dark House." The kid's eyes gleamed with excitement in the darkness, even as the bloodshot veins in the whites screamed he needed something.

"Mayor?"

"Yeah."

"You good to get it?"

"Yeah." He squirmed in the seat, his hand reaching out to rub the soft leather. Caleb was obviously trying to figure out how much money Charlie actually made.

"I've got a favor to ask." Charlie reached into the console next to him, and with a click it opened, and he withdrew two baggies of white powder. It was the last of this batch that he'd "fixed" six months ago. "One for him, and one for you."

The kid's eyes squinted as Charlie held them out. "What's the catch?"

"You don't use yours until you've given the other one to the mayor." A sober person would ask what was wrong with the drugs, but this kid hadn't been sober in a year. "After he gets his, go get yours."

"That's it?"

"Yup. I want to spread a little love tonight. I'm feeling ... charitable."

"Sweet." The baggies disappeared into his pocket, and Caleb vanished out the door. Charlie took a deep breath of sweet air after he'd left.

"We can go home now, Luther. Thank you."

CHAPTER FOUR

Charlie spent the next few days reacquainting himself with his dick. He hadn't masturbated since he was younger, and the ladies of the night he typically employed no longer held the appeal they once had. Granted, they'd actually become friends of his, and even Lola, his long-time go-to, knew something was up with him.

Luther had a thing for her anyway. Charlie had figured that out recently and stopped using her. But tonight, even her best cohorts weren't doing it for him. He tried to think of one woman who worked in Lola's establishment that could get him off, and his best option was himself.

Because he couldn't stop thinking about Amelia.

In his sterile bachelor pad, the penthouse apartment that someone else had decorated for him, he lay on his bed, shirtless, thinking about her. Wondering what her bedroom looked like. Imagining what she slept in. Picturing her doing things to herself.

That wasn't the best idea, but he couldn't stop himself. He visualized her touching herself, twisting her nipples, slapping her clit.

"Fuck," he muttered to himself. Of course, he imagined her on silk sheets, because her skin was flawless and the complementary textures did something to him. He pictured her totally naked, because he could. In his mind's eye, she rolled over on the bed, her tits squashing to either side, her ass in the air, the puckered virgin rosebud crying out to him. Her ass wanted him to destroy it, as only he could do.

"Jesus Christ." Charlie got out of bed, hating himself for thinking of her this way. It was a fantasy, and he was only making things worse for himself by bringing her up to his office. It was one thing to fuck one of his whores and think of her while he did it. It was another altogether to smell her scent filling his inner sanctuary while he tried to work.

He stalked to the kitchen and filled a glass of ice-cold water, gulping it down as he stood at the counter, picturing her bent over it, crying out his name while he pounded into her.

Charlie prowled around his apartment, seeing her everywhere. Splayed out on the black leather sofa, beseeching him with her eyes. She was in his workout room, bending at the waist to pick up dumbbells from the floor. Amelia was in his rarely used home office, spread-eagle on the desk, glistening pussy weeping with need for him.

Amelia was everywhere in his empty space.

He finally made it to his bathroom, where a shower was his only hope to get her out of his system enough to go to bed.

Soaping up his dick, he stroked it from base to tip, giving in to his fantasies. His hands were too big, but he managed to suspend reality enough to pretend it was her stroking him, gripping his balls tight.

When he came, he immediately wanted to do it again, but managed to suppress the urge. He'd gotten the edge off; surely he could sleep now.

**

Amelia checked on Gram while her coffee brewed. Her one luxury was a nice coffee pot in this tiny house. Everything else was secondhand or a relic of Gram's past. The refrigerator and stove were avocado green; the kitchen furniture was all purchased when the house was new. The living room furniture the next year, covered in quilts and afghans that Gram had made over the years. The walls were covered in pictures Gram and her husband had taken of family vacations and stuff. Her grandmother hadn't changed anything when she'd moved in after her divorce.

But Amelia had insisted on a new coffee pot. Nobody else drank coffee. Gram heated water for her tea in the microwave, since

Amelia unplugged the stove every morning before she left for work. Hell, most of the time, she didn't plug it in when she came home, so the relic was rarely used.

Amelia's weakness was coffee. She loved the earthy flavors, and her monthly extravagant self-love purchases were at a coffee shop down the street from where she worked. They had a great Italian roast that she enjoyed for her early mornings, and another she liked for her café au lait on the weekends.

Gram was still sleeping. That was fine. It was only six a.m. Amelia put a tray on her bedside table and turned on the lamp.

"Time to wake up, Gram. I have to get ready to go to work. I've brought your tea." It was toast and marmalade, a cup of tea with cream and sugar, and some butter cookies she'd found at the grocery store. Not a high tea by any stretch of the imagination, but it made Gram happy to have it.

"I had the most wonderful dreams, but I can't remember them." Gram blinked sleepily.

"Do you need me to change anything?" Amelia asked tentatively. One of her least favorite jobs was changing Gram's sleeping diapers, but she was more than willing.

"No dear. I can do it." Gram managed to sit on the side of the bed while Amelia went to her room to change into work clothes—a skirt and jacket combo that was shorter than she would have liked, but looked better on her than she thought when she saw it on the hanger. The sales associate had made her try it on, and it was, in fact, perfect. And the color brought out her eyes and made her look …

… vivacious.

That wasn't a word she had ever used on herself, but these new clothes gave her an energy she hadn't had before. She felt more professional wearing them, and less like a child playing dress-up.

Going back to check on Gram, she found her back in bed, wearing a different nightie. She sat up with her tray in her lap and a book to her side. *Reclaimed by the Rake.* She was set for the day. A short honk told her Luther was here. She rolled her eyes.

"I left a sandwich in the ice box for you. I'll see you tonight?"

"Yes, dear. I hope you have a lovely engagement."

Amelia walked down the hallway, past the faded wallpaper and photos, wondering, not for the first time, if living somewhere different would take Gram out of the past. The woman lived in Regency England, and Amelia understood why. She eyeballed Gram's wedding photo as she walked past it.

Her husband had beaten her a lot before he died. Gram didn't talk about it much, but the mean glint in his eyes was visible even on his wedding day, as if he couldn't wait to get home and hurt his new wife.

Amelia wondered if it was something in her genes that had attracted her to Jackson.

Gathering her coffee in her travel mug, she strapped her bag over her shoulder and left the house to get in the car as Luther held the door open.

If she could afford someplace else for Gram, she would move her in a heartbeat. But unless this new job worked out really, really well, she didn't have a hope of someplace new anytime soon.

This house was paid for. She could barely afford the taxes on it; she certainly couldn't afford a new home.

Traffic was light, as it had been for a few days. She couldn't help but wonder if Charlie was a good luck charm in that regard.

The long drive gave her the time to embrace her feelings for Charlie and indulge in them. She enjoyed the way her nipples tightened and her core got warm. He was a unique specimen of man, and she loved the way he made her feel. Of course, she had to be careful with those feelings, because she knew it was a crush and could be nothing else. He was her boss, and she needed this job to work.

But she could let herself get a little carried away on her drive in. As long as she didn't act on anything, she was fine.

Right?

Shaking her head a little, Amelia realized she was there. Mentally ticking off what she had to do before Charlie made it in to work, she remembered today was coffee maker day.

Amelia smiled. It would be a good day.

CHAPTER FIVE

That morning, Charlie was late to work after a late night. He wasn't used to having anyone notice when he was on time or late or whatever, and today should have been no exception. But when he walked in, Amelia was in her usual spot at her desk, looking fresh-faced and lovely. The image stabbed him in the chest with a dagger.

He shook his head at himself and proceeded to his office, removing his suit coat as he went. Her inhale was audible, and he smirked to himself. That was one thing that made him notice her in the front lobby all those months ago: her inability to take her eyes off him when he entered. He didn't need ego boosts, generally, but from her, it was definitely welcome. She was so damn nice and innocent. It was lovely to imagine defiling her.

"Your new coffee maker is being delivered today. Just thought you would want to know about it."

"Good, thank you." He didn't need a damn coffee maker, but like everything else, she wasn't doing this halfway.

An hour later, he realized just how thorough she was.

A young guy, with an eyebrow piercing and tattoos all over his arms, showed up with a huge box on a dolly. Charlie watched as he rolled it in, leaned against it, had Amelia sign something, then actually flirted with her.

The body language was astounding. How could a self-respecting man be so damn transparent? He shut his laptop and watched as the douchebag made a joke he couldn't hear.

Amelia laughed. Actually giggled. She didn't hide her smile from this guy. Or her laugh. She simply did it, with zero thought to the repercussions.

Charlie was livid. Unable to help himself, he stood and strode out into the main room.

"It goes in there," he said, pointing to the lounge area. "You can unbox it and leave." His words were short and clipped and he watched with satisfaction as the guy rushed to do his bidding. While the guy was in the lounge, Charlie turned on Amelia.

She looked at him with wide eyes, and her mouth dropped open. He had an image of himself shoving his cock in that mouth and grabbing her hair and fucking the surprise right off her face.

But he didn't.

Instead, he spun on his heel and walked back into his office, slamming the door. Amelia stayed behind her desk until the guy left, giving him a small wave.

Charlie had no idea why this little wisp of a woman was taking up so much of his mental energy. She always had, but now she was in his domain, coming into his office every day and *owning* things. He was flabbergasted. Her mark was everywhere, her scent, her eyes, bringing a shadowy light into his darkness.

But where his shadows were the absence of light, her shadows were light, the sun filtering through the shade of trees. She was life, he was death, but he needed her here.

It wasn't like he was going to do anything about her. He'd thought just bringing her here and helping her out of a shitty situation in the lobby would be enough. But he found himself wanting more.

He wanted to know her sins, what scared her, whether or not she cried at night. He wanted to be her priest, hear her darkest confessions.

He tried not to watch her as she piddled around the lounge area, but his damn windows everywhere inhibited that. He couldn't help but see her.

So when she got on her hands and knees to plug the monstrosity of a coffee maker into the outlet under the cabinet, he couldn't help himself.

The next thing he knew, he was leaning against the doorway to the lounge area, willing her skirt to fly off so he could see the round globes of her pert little ass. Vaguely, he wondered what sort of panties she was wearing. Would it be a G-string? Or something silky, with lace around the edges? Or pure lace, where the outlines of what was underneath would tempt him?

He watched her, completely enraptured, as she wriggled out from underneath the cabinet with an erotic grunt, then saw him.

She squealed and fell on her rump, and he smiled at her discomfiture.

"I didn't mean to scare you." He planted his feet, not willing to break his composure and take her like he wanted. He knew full well if he helped her off the ground, he would help her over the countertop as he raised her skirts and plunged balls deep into her from behind. He'd been dreaming about it too much to hold back.

"It's okay," she stammered as she rose to her feet. She wasn't the least bit graceful, and he was rewarded with a flash of garters, stockings, and pink silk panties that he would take with him to bed tonight.

He cleared his throat, saving the image for later. "What is that thing?"

"It's a coffee maker," she replied proudly, gesturing to it like a game show hostess. "I put myself through part of college as a barista, so I know what a good coffee maker entails. Unfortunately, the industrial Bunn you had in here collecting dust need not apply for the position."

He didn't miss the little nugget of information. She hadn't finished college. At least, not as a barista at a coffee shop.

"What did you go to college for?" He dealt in information, and while part of the question was habit, Charlie couldn't resist learning anything about her.

"Oh," she said in a nonchalant way that didn't fool Charlie one iota. "I just got some basics out of the way. General Ed. Nothing else." He didn't miss the shadow that flitted over her eyes, and he smiled. There was pain there, and while he didn't want her to hurt, he still felt like he had another piece of her puzzle.

She'd turned her back and was wiping a countertop, effectively ending the conversation. Definitely pain there.

But Charlie wasn't done. He wanted to hear her voice some more. "What makes a good cup of coffee?"

Spinning back around she gave him a grin, and he relished the brightness. It banished the shadows from her eyes. Granted, he loved those shadows, but seeing her without them for once, was … nice. And all about a cup of coffee.

Amelia spun around and began extolling the features of the coffee pot, the seemingly most important being the correct temperature for brewing. He listened with half an ear, while imagining her in her underwear.

"Here. I'll make you one."

He grunted in agreement, not giving a shit about a cup of coffee, but wanting her to continue talking to him about something she was apparently passionate about, because it made her so damn *alive*.

She flitted and floated around the room, moving to a refrigerator he hadn't noticed before for some milk.

"When did we get a fridge in here?"

She looked at him, one eyebrow quirked. "Yesterday. You were here."

"I must have been actually working. Did you flirt with that delivery guy, too?" He could have swallowed a gun for admitting he'd noticed her flirting and might actually be jealous. He hadn't even admitted the thought to himself. Until now. But yeah, he was jealous of that punk-ass motherfucker who'd smiled at her.

"It was the same guy, and I suppose I did. I was just being friendly. It was a lot of work for him to bring that up here. But he did tell me about the freight elevator, which I started using yesterday, and I like it so much better than the glass one."

She babbled on, while she did something with the milk. Steaming it, he supposed. She was making a damn fancy cup of fucking coffee.

"You don't like the glass elevator?"

She shrugged. "No. I don't like heights." Then she walked over to him and handed him a coffee mug filled with a rich smelling aroma of good coffee. He stared at it. The solar system was in his coffee cup.

"What's this?"

She giggled at him again, and his eyes immediately went to her mouth.

"It's a latte. Steamed milk and espresso."

"But you put fucking Saturn in there." He was gobsmacked.

"That's microfoam from the steamed milk. It's really finely textured…" She continued babbling about the different kinds of foam for different coffees, and he was entranced by her. Once again, she was passionately talking about something, and he could only imagine her talking to him about her passions all day long.

And all night. Lying in bed, propped up on his chest and talking about coffee.

What the actual fuck?

To distract himself, he took a tentative sip. He usually drank his coffee black, from his simple little Mr. Coffee drip maker at home before coming in. Who knew his mind would be blown by one of these fancy little fuckers?

He licked his lips where he could feel the foam and was satisfied she seemed as mesmerized by the movement as he was by her garters.

"It's good." He was staring at her over the rim of his cup, trying to figure out what to do with her. Should he bed her and get it over with? Or should he push her away and stop this nonsense? He certainly didn't see himself making love to her and proposing they have a life together. But he suddenly had the sensation she would change him, irrevocably. He was interested by her when she worked the lobby. Enough so that he had her employment papers and a list of places she could shop at the ready to hire her. In the short amount of time she'd been in his offices though, he'd become slightly obsessed with her.

Charlie supposed he would just continue along the same vein as he had this week, until Cayman. Maybe then something would present itself. Meanwhile, he needed to eat. It was well past lunch time, and he was hungry.

He gulped down the drink that was surely supposed to be savored and sipped, enjoying the look of disappointment on her face. He'd already fucked up Saturn with his first sip; what did she expect?

The disappointment turned to something else as he lowered his mug and handed it back to her. It was the darkness again, as her eyes squinted at him.

"Did you hear about the Mayor? He died last night. They say it's an overdose." Her words were quiet, but she continued forcing them across her tongue. "It was all over the news on the radio on my ride in." She licked her lips, staring at his.

The darkness was beautiful. Shadows of suspicion crossing the green orbs of her eyes. Directed at him. It made his cock twitch in his pants, and he knew he needed to get out of there. He was about to lose control with her. And her veiled suspicions only told him she was smart, and he might need to be careful with her.

Or not. What sort of darkness could he get from Amelia Flores if he wasn't careful? Tempting. So damn tempting.

"Yeah, I heard about it. Such a shame."

He opened his mouth to invite her with him to lunch, then shut it. No. The status quo must remain. He was doing well for himself. No need to fuck it up with a woman.

Besides, he wanted to do some networking at a new restaurant in town. And he needed to banish the thoughts of her delicious darkness.

CHAPTER SIX

He was late for the lunch rush, so he seated himself at the bar. It was an old world style, with burnished wood countertops, low lighting, and glassware everywhere. The mirror behind the bar was stacked with shelves of liquor and the bartender wore a black polo shirt with the word Nonna's on the breast. A TV in the corner had the local news on it, but he didn't need to hear it. He knew what they were talking about.

It was casual class and made him wonder if there was something here he could use.

"Scotch on the rocks, please. Whatever top shelf you have." He slid onto a stool a couple of chairs down from a large man with a short beard. Neither of them spoke at first, Charlie nursing his drink and looking at a menu while the other guy silently drank his drink—something clear that made him grimace with each sip.

Charlie ordered a plate of antipasto and sat back to think on his current situation. His business would survive whatever bullshit Forrester was tossing around, it always did. Bascom Forrester was one of those guys who got to the top purely by luck. Charlie had done his research, years ago, and discounted the man's brain a long time ago. He was dumber than a sack full of rocks.

Sure, he knew when to get rid of competition and knew who to buy off, but he was sloppy and would get caught by the wrong guy eventually. His only saving grace was his brother high up in the police force, who saved his ass on more than one occasion. Eventually his brother's own aspirations would come out ahead, and Forrester would be done.

Charlie didn't have designs on the title of king of the underworld, or whatever. Forrester just got in the way of his business, an awful lot. It would be nice to get that wrinkle out of the way.

His meal arrived and he speared random foods with a fork while his mind turned to Amelia, a more pleasant distraction.

Charlie had been fascinated by her since he'd first seen her, a surreal light in the darkness of his life. He'd watch her out of the corner of his eye as he strode through the lobby, then more obviously through the glass of the elevator as it ascended to his office floor. She was so innocent, so naively optimistic, so … friendly.

And now she worked for him and he didn't have to be subtle as he watched her. It was his prerogative as her boss, to make sure she was doing her job, right?

That's what he told himself anyway. Besides, he enjoyed watching her work, especially when she did something she enjoyed, like messing around with that stupid coffee maker.

Who knew coffee would make her so happy? Was it the coffee, though, or just the fact she was so intimately knowledgeable about the making of it? Did she love being an expert on the coffee? Some people were like that. It didn't matter, just as long as they knew more about something than the other person. She didn't seem that way, though.

But was it just the coffee?

"A woman?" A voice spoke, low and gravelly, next to him. He jerked around to see the bearded guy talking to him.

"What?"

"You here because of a woman?"

The man behind the bar laughed as he polished a glass. "Who isn't?"

"Not specifically, no, but I was thinking about one." Charlie admitted as he caught himself smiling like a dumbass. No wonder the dude had spoken up. He was probably over here sighing like a teenaged girl.

"She worth it?" He made a face like the one he'd been making when he took a drink. Charlie wondered if his drink was that bad, or if the woman he was thinking of was that smooth. He almost chuckled at the thought.

"Worth what?" Charlie pushed his finished plate away, wondering where all the food had gone. He guessed he'd been so lost in thought, he'd just been on autopilot. A bit of a shame. He had no idea if the food was any good or not. The guy behind the bar took it and dumped it in a tub near the end of the bar, coming back to polish the glasses again.

"It, man. Is she worth *it?* A lot of women aren't. Just make sure she's worth it before you go investing all sorts of energy into something she's going to just throw away." His voice had degraded into a growly snarl that spoke of an ages-old heartbreak.

Charlie mused over the guy's condition. His clothing that wasn't fancy, but he wasn't totally disheveled. He probably wasn't a regular drunk. Charlie read him like a book. He was here for heartbreak, to drown sorrows, but his words spoke of a long reflection. Some time had passed and he was reminiscing.

"Anniversary?" Charlie asked, just to see if he was right.

"Yup." The guy finished his drink and motioned for another. The bartender got him one, slowly, as if he didn't really want to serve him another. Charlie pushed his glass toward him and made eye contact. "It's the last one though. I'm done giving her energy, because she wasn't worth it."

"Wasn't?" He didn't know why he was prodding so much. He wasn't sure he cared about this drunk stranger's love history, except he was curious. He didn't have much experience, and with Amelia in the forefront of his mind, he needed any excuse to not do the things he wanted to do to her.

"She's dead. He killed her." He took another sip, made another face, set his drink down on the bartop.

Intrigued, and smelling a potential job, Charlie turned to face the guy.

"Okay, now I'm curious. Start at the beginning, since you brought all this up." He opened his posture, an old body language trick to get clients to give him information.

He sighed and his shoulders drooped in what looked like defeat. "We married young. She wasn't ready to settle down, but I went off to Iraq and she stayed home. When I came back, she was different and wanted a divorce. For some stupid reason, I wouldn't give it to her, thinking she needed to fall in love with me again. But she was having an affair, and she left me for him. What neither of us knew was that he didn't want her in any sort of permanent way. She thought he would leave his wife for her, and he didn't realize she was leaving me for him until she told him she was going to. So instead of breaking up with her, he killed her. So I'm reading a Dear John letter while she's wrapping her car around a tree trunk."

His words were slurred and spoken slowly, but there was a strength behind them that told Charlie it was a story he hadn't told in a while but had thought about frequently. It was harsh, for sure. He wasn't sure what to say, except if this was the guy's last time to consciously dwell on it, he needed to get it all out.

And Charlie was a nosy fucker.

"How do you know he killed her? Couldn't it have been an accident?" He knew of all people that it was hard to fix a car so it would stop working and cause an accident. Not impossible, just hard.

"I was her mechanic. I had just tuned the fucking thing up two weeks before that. It was an old Camaro with T-tops. The only thing she fucking loved. Except Bascom." He spat the word Bascom like it was phlegm.

Charlie almost choked. "Bascom Forrester?"

"You know him?"

"By reputation." And the fact his best friend had plotted his demise for years. Finishing up his Scotch, Charlie saw this as his cue to leave. He pulled out a card. "Hey, I'm Charlie Delmonico. My driver can take you home when you're ready."

"Yeah, sure." His head sank lower. "I'm Dean Davis, by the way." They shook hands and Charlie clapped him on the back as he pulled out his phone, watching him leave.

He called the office, telling Amelia he wouldn't be in this afternoon, as a meeting had suddenly come up. He asked her to look up Dean's phone number, then he called his friend Adam.

Aside from Luther, Adam was his only real friend. Oldest too. They had all ended up in the same group home, and Adam had loved telling him he would end up some Neighborhood Watch asshole, or the president of his kids' PTO. Charlie had always meddled.

Of course, he wasn't part of any neighborhood bullshit, and the PTO was so far off his radar it wasn't even funny. He was too fucking dark. If he was on a PTO, he'd probably put hits out on anybody that bullied his kid or some shit.

Although the thought of kids was sort of laughable. It didn't matter if he wanted them; Charlie was not father material.

"Hey, man." Adam answered on the first ring.

"You down for a drink? I'm at that new place uptown. Nonna's?"

"I'll be there in twenty. You sending Luther?"

"Nope. I've got him doing something else." Charlie tossed his credit card on the bar and motioned to Dean. He spoke to Dean, jutting his chin toward the door. "Hey, man, see you later, 'kay?" Dean took the hint and gave him a thumbs-up as he stumbled toward the door. The bartender gave him a grateful look.

Adam chuckled and hung up.

The bartender refilled his glass and set a basket of bread in front of him.

"Thanks for that. He's been coming in this week, which is cool, cuz I want some regulars. New place and all." He shrugged and spread his hands. "But at the same time, I wasn't sure if it would piss him off to cut him off at one thirty in the afternoon or not. I'm no wimp"—he gave a small flex—"but that dude is huge. He hadn't gotten this drunk until today." He took a deep breath. "Still trying to figure all this out. Guess I need a bigger bartender."

"You own the place?"

He grinned and held out his hand. "Me and my brother. I'm Luca. The regular bartender doesn't start until the dinner rush. We're all filling in everywhere, trying to figure out regular jobs."

Charlie shook his hand and noted the strong grip. "Charlie."

"I heard. Your name is familiar. What do you do? You work around here?" Luca leaned on the bar slightly.

"I have an office in the Transylvania tower. I help people with problems that come up." Charlie used the nickname given by the locals to his building. He actually owned it, but not many people knew that. He hadn't renamed it the Delmonico Tower or anything. Right now, it had the generic title of the Haines building, named after the architect who constructed it a century ago, right before he tossed himself from the roof during the stock market crash.

Luca grinned. "Like a fixer?"

"Something like that."

Adam chose that moment to walk in, wearing his customary suit, looking around appraisingly. He seemed to approve as he settled onto a stool next to him and ordered a gin old-fashioned. That was his customary test of any new bar. What poor Luca didn't know was that Adam was going to judge harshly as to whether or not the entire restaurant was up to his standards based on this one drink.

"You want the traditional recipe, or one with a twist?" Luca apparently saw the weight of the drink in Adam's eyes, which were narrowed on him at the question.

"Let's go with the traditional this time. You pull out a blow torch and I'm leaving."

Charlie smiled as he heard the exchange. Sometimes, he wanted his buddy to lighten up, but other times, he took an enormous amount of joy in watching him make people sweat.

But Luca wasn't fazed. With a shrug, he took some cherries and peeled an orange slice and got started. He muddled them expertly with some syrup before pouring the gin in, tapping in the bitters, and topping it with a lemon peel.

Adam sipped it before nodding his approval. "You know, they used the fruit to hide the taste of the prohibition moonshine."

"Yep. I did know that. In fact, this is the original cocktail. Or pretty close to it," Luca said as he tossed a towel over his shoulder. "You guys good for a minute? I need to go check the kitchen."

Charlie nodded to the guy as he left, thankful for the privacy.

"So, I met a guy—" Charlie began, but Adam interrupted with a laugh. He ignored it, knowing Adam would sober up quickly. "Who has a hard-on for Forrester almost as big as yours." Luca had come back almost immediately, clearly not needed in the kitchen.

"I don't know, did he have the dude's wife kidnapped?" Adam's face was skeptical, but Luca managed to subdue his double take. Charlie noticed it, even if Adam didn't.

"He had this guy's wife killed."

"Okay, I'll give you that one." Charlie had yet to be directly affected on a personal level by Forrester's actions, but he was well aware of the guy's douche-baggery.

Luca spun around and faced them, all pretenses with the bar towel gone. His fists clenched as his jaw ticked.

"You guys seem powerful enough to take him down, with enough muscle behind you." He spoke the words on a low growl, and Charlie noticed Adam's thoughtful look.

"What's it to you?" Adam asked.

"He killed my parents."

Charlie looked at Adam, who looked back at him. They'd been talking for years about a plan to get rid of Bascom Forrester, but killing him was too good. Nope, the plans they had required a shit ton of money and a lot of muscle.

With Luca and Dean on board, it might be doable.

"You know, I've hired this guy to work my security at the warehouse. He has a history with Forrester too. We could have a circle jerk with all the hard-ons."

Charlie flinched at the mental image Adam put in his head.

"Let's get a meeting together and pound out some details. You in?" he asked, turning to Luca.

"Name a time and a place and I'll be there."

"Nobody talk until I come up with a plan."

"What about this guy?" Adam was talking about Luca. "How do you know you can trust him?"

Charlie looked at Luca. Aside from seeming like a nice guy, he couldn't really. Not any more than anybody else.

"Because he knows what I do for a living, and he knows that if he talks, I can have his restaurant shut down and have him personally ruined." Blackmail was Charlie's stock and trade. Why not use it for personal gain? He chuckled to himself, not really sure if he knew how *not* to blackmail people.

"Point taken. Drinks are on the house." He headed back to the kitchen.

"You certainly have a way with people," Adam pointed out, sipping his drink.

"That's why I'm good at what I do."

CHAPTER SEVEN

"Why are you still here?" He seemed angry, with his downturned mouth and the set of his jaw. Her discovery of yesterday afternoon was still on her mind, and she knew he wasn't a man to anger. He was a killer. A man who made things happen. His friendliness at times notwithstanding, she'd seen him irritated at the delivery boy, and did *not* want to see him full-on angry at her.

"I'm still working on this." She shrugged as she clicked the mouse and saved the file. "No reason for me not to." She remembered the task he'd called to give her this afternoon. "Oh. I found that guy's number you wanted." She handed him a slip of paper he shoved in his pocket without looking at.

"I'm taking you home."

His words were simple, yet the authority in them was unquestionable. Except she had no idea what he meant. She couldn't go to his home. There was no way. Was that why he was paying her so much money? To go home with him? Amelia squeaked in response, then felt the flames in her face as she opened her mouth to protest.

"Not my home." He sighed heavily. His impatience with her was clear in the tight frown on his face. "I'll take you to your home. I don't want to wait for Luther to come back from taking you. It will be easier for me."

"Oh, you don't have to do that. I live outside the city limits. It's almost an hour. I can get a cab." Her yawn interrupted her own words, and she covered her mouth. "Sorry. That was rude." Still, did she want him knowing where she lived?

Oh hell, if he was as powerful as she thought, he already knew.

"And illustrating my point perfectly. I have a driver who has had at least two naps today." He held out his arm to usher her in front of him as he opened the door. "Let's go."

**

She was a hard worker; that's for sure. Certainly harder than the idiot he'd hired two years ago, before deciding if he needed arm candy for an assignment, he'd get an escort. That woman had used his money to refurbish her wardrobe, and then been a vapid beast to get rid of. Somewhere along the line she'd gotten designs to become Mrs. Delmonico and that was it. Charlie had fired her with a severance package she didn't deserve.

But Amelia had done more work in a week than that other one had done in the month he'd had her on his payroll. He was delighted.

Of course, it was really difficult to work with the distraction of her, but he supposed he would get used to her. The novelty would wear off, and he'd be productive again.

Charlie's underworld contacts were frustrating him, demanding more and more money for their information. They were more afraid of Forrester, and Charlie knew he had to make an example of someone to get some contacts' attention. Hopefully, Desert Eagle's death would get some of his cronies to give Charlie the information he needed right now.

Charlie marveled at the difference in the way Amelia rubbed the leather on his seats from the way the kid had, last night. The chains of Caleb's addictions had his fingers rubbing with greed, as Amelia's innocence had her rubbing it with wonder at the softness. Charlie wagered she hadn't factored the cost of it into her thoughts at all, while that was obviously all Caleb had cared about.

Safely ensconced in the obscurity of his back seat, he put those thoughts out of his head. They were too dark to be thought of in the lightness that was Amelia. He realized he wanted to talk to her, see if she could dispel the shadows inside him. Or maybe she would say something to make herself less attractive. That might be better. It was stupid, but maybe she would slip up and be silly or thoughtless or something unattractive and he'd see some damn sense.

"So, do you live alone?" If there were no roommates, maybe a quick fuck would get her out of his system.

"I live with Graham. It's just us two." Huh. Boyfriend. Or husband. Whatever. But instead of the name helping with things and taking her off the table, he reacted viscerally in an entirely unexpected and inappropriate way.

A pain radiated from his jaw and he realized he was clenching it tightly, grinding his molars. No wonder she hadn't wanted to travel for nearly a week. There was a man at home who would pine for her. And probably vice versa. The thought alone had the shadows inside him gaining strength, morphing into something dangerous.

He clenched his fists, and glutton for punishment that he was, pursued the line of questioning. "Graham?"

"Actually," she yawned again, and Charlie briefly wondered if *Graham* could unwind her the way he wanted to. Probably not. "It's Great Gram. My grandma died a few years back. So it's just the two of us in her house."

Charlie swam in the relief he felt and it was uncomfortable. He didn't like it.

At all.

Emotions were for the weak. And he wasn't weak. These feelings were handicaps. Jealousy. Relief he had nothing to be jealous of. He couldn't afford that in his line of business.

He hadn't had emotions since his mother had been alive. That was the last time he could remember feeling any sort of innocent joy or happiness. Now, here was Amelia, making him feel like he should deserve the warm fuzzies about her great-grandma or whatever.

"Close your eyes and rest. Luther has your address. I'll wake you when we get there."

She tried to resist, that much was obvious. But she was also tired, probably from her commute and long hours in his office, so that made it his fault. Before long, she had her head leaned on his shoulder, her mouth wide open, and soft snores coming from her.

The weight of her head was grounding, as if providing her a shoulder to lean on was a salve to his wounds. He didn't resist the pull to touch her hair, and it was indeed as soft as he'd been imagining. Weaving his fingers into the sleek bun she had at the back of her neck, he tugged it out, watching it fall in waves over her shoulder.

She leaned into him, slouching across his shoulder and down his chest, until after one final adjustment, she'd curled up in the seat and had her head on his lap. By the time they'd reached the ancient suburb she lived in, there was a thin string of saliva dangling from her mouth and pooling on his slacks. Decidedly unchaste thoughts rolled through his head.

The neighborhood she lived in was a throwback from the Korean War, when this was all Army housing. The single-family dwellings were tiny, and most still had the asbestos siding on them, but they pulled up to one that had aluminum siding and bright, cheery flowered window boxes. An old rocking chair sat on the porch. It was quaint. And fit Amelia to a tee.

"We're there," he murmured as he stroked her cheek. Jesus, she was soft. He had no business wanting her like he did. He would only ruin her, as was evidenced by his thoughts about her drool and its proximity to his dick, and how badly he wanted her drool on his dick, preferably lubricating her mouth.

Or her ass. That was a comforting thought. Charlie was an ass man, always had been. He was glad Amelia had come to work in his offices, as it gave him a great view of her ass on occasion. He imagined sliding between the sweet globes on a daily basis.

These thoughts soothed him. He knew she would never let him have her ass, so the unrealistic expectations actually grounded him in some sort of reality. The dichotomy of his fantasies versus her reality reminded him of who he was and who she was.

"Oh good." She interrupted the feral direction his thoughts had turned and raised her head just as his erection was about to poke her in the cheek. "I'm so sorry!" Amelia was realizing where her head had just been, and was a lovely shade of red.

Thankfully, she didn't try to wipe away the pool of her slobber, or else there would be no doubt as to the direction of his thoughts. As it was, there was a visible evidence, but thankfully the car was dark.

"No worries, I'll walk you in." He had a morbid fascination with where she lived. He needed to see it.

"O-kay." She grabbed her purse and the enormous bag she insisted on carrying with her and led the way to the porch where she stopped and fumbled with her keys. "You can go. I'll be fine."

Now that he was closer, he saw the siding was dirty and the flowers were plastic. Cheery-looking from the street, but up close, they were drab and used.

"I want to see where you live," he said simply, and she shrugged, opening her door and going inside.

"Nobody ever tells you no, do they?" Amelia was muttering to herself, but he chuckled at her words.

It was the truth. Nobody ever said no to him, and he liked it that way.

The inside of the house was dark, aside from a small lamp next to the couch. It was worn, yet covered in a crocheted coverlet that reminded him of his foster parents. The first ones. He rarely thought of them, the times too happy to remember without feeling things he didn't want to explore.

"I need to warn you. If you're meeting Gram, she's not in … the real world." Amelia stood in a doorway that led to a small hallway, twining her hands together before giving him a sigh and turning to go down it. He could hear her as she spoke in a soothing voice. "Gram? It's Amelia. Did you eat?"

He looked around, and being nosy, rifled through a pile of papers on the kitchen table, which could plainly be seen from where he had stood by the front door, even though it was in the backside of the house. Papers and Mason jars. The table was covered in them.

This place was tiny.

There was a pink slip of paper announcing a foreclosure for back taxes. He pulled it out of the stack, reading it quickly, then returning it to the stack and going to find Amelia.

"Oh, it was lovely. I wish you could have gone with me."

"Shameful that I didn't. When I was a girl on the ton, one didn't go gallivanting about without a chaperone. It was scandalous." Amelia sat on the side of a bed holding a frail woman with a nightgown with buttons all the way to the neck and a ruffle on top. She looked like her skin was made of paper, as the gown seemed thicker than her skin. "Oh! Who is this charmingly handsome fellow?" Striking blue eyes found him across the room and twinkled in the lamplight.

"Charlie Delmonico, ma'am," he immediately responded, seeing what was expected. He took the hand she held out and delicately kissed the knuckle that smelled like cold cream. It was a familiar smell, again reminding him of his first foster mother. "It's a pleasure to meet you." He laid it on thick, and the woman tittered in response. Certainly not in the real world. It had been a long time since someone had *tittered* at him. Someone he hadn't paid for the company, anyway.

"Okay, Gram, I'll leave you to go to sleep then. I'm home. I'll see you in the morning." Amelia kissed her gram's forehead fondly and then tucked her blankets up on her chin before turning off the lamp. Charlie watched the bed shift as Gram rolled over to her side with a grunt.

"She does nothing but read Regency romance novels, and that's sort of the world where she lives." Amelia walked the three steps down the hallway to the living room. Charlie looked at the closed door at the other end of the hallway, knowing that had to be where Amelia slept. He resisted the urge to open the door and check it out. "That and pickles. She makes pickles and reads all day."

Amelia opened the fridge door and started removing stacks of pickle jars that matched the Mason jars on the table, only these actually had pickles in them.

He must have looked as confused as he felt.

"They're refrigerator pickles. No cooking involved, which is good, because I turn the gas off when I'm not home so she can't cook. We had a rather alarming kitchen fire a couple of years ago, and that's when I learned the trick. Every day she makes pickles, and every night, I throw them out so she can do it again tomorrow." Amelia was babbling and something warm swelled inside him. He liked hearing her.

Charlie came to a decision right then and there. It was something he should have asked about, or at least been intuitive enough to figure out before now.

"Sleep in tomorrow and come in whenever. I won't be in the office anyway. Get Gram sorted for your new schedule. I'll have a nurse brought in for while you're at work." Before he examined his motives too much, he dropped a kiss on her forehead, similar to her kiss on Gram's and left the house as quickly as he could. He did not want to think about what had just happened there, the depth of things he was sinking into.

CHAPTER EIGHT

Amelia slept in until seven a.m. and rose feeling rested and rejuvenated. Even though the weekend was two days away, she still felt like she could do anything. And she would. Working her hours, as far away as she did, meant she didn't have downtime ever, during regular office hours. She'd saved enough from her shopping spree that she could afford to pay off some bills that had been plaguing her for a while. In fact, she was making today take care of tax bill day.

She drove to the tax office first thing.

But when she got to the tax office, her bill was paid already. In the dingy government office, the exhausted-looking woman at the counter told her impatiently that it was paid. She did offer a small smile as she looked at her computer screen. "Just in time, too."

Confused, she drove to Mr. McGee's house in a daze. He was a farmer who lived a mile from the house and kept Gram in cucumbers when they were in season. In the mornings, Mr. McGee would drop off a bushel basket of cucumbers for Gram every couple of days so she could pickle. Amelia had yet to figure out why pickling was so important to her gram, only that it was. She had to keep fresh jars and lots of ingredients for her to pickle with, or else everyone would pay the price.

Later that day, she was in her room packing for the Cayman Islands, while Gram messed around in the kitchen. Mr. Delmonico had said six days, so she packed all three bathing suits, none of which she was looking forward to wearing. They were way skimpier than she was accustomed to. Also, she packed sun dresses, shorts, the pajamas the saleslady had picked out which were sexier than anything she owned, a formal gown, and blouses, including shoes for everything. Luckily she'd bought luggage to pack it all in. A matching set.

It was crazy how much her life had changed in the last few days. Yet, as she heard Gram puttering around in the kitchen, the comforting sounds of her singing to herself while she screwed lids onto jars reminded her it was all still essentially the same.

Just more expensive. The nurse was due here any moment, and she hoped the lady would get along with Gram. Charlie had texted this morning to let Amelia know to expect her.

He fixed problems. He was fixing her life. That's when it dawned on her.

He'd paid her tax bill.

It had to be him. It all made sense. She'd been in a shitty job, in the lobby on display for the world to see. Mr. Delmonico had seen and for some reason, swooped in and given her a better job, paying her exponentially more money. He'd bought her all new clothes, promised her trips to exotic locations, gotten a nurse for Gram, and paid the tax bill that had been looming over her head.

What the hell?

What did he expect from her in return? She looked at the lacy, silky underwear the saleslady had insisted on, and it suddenly dawned on her.

Charlie Delmonico had bought her. Signed sealed and delivered.

And she'd signed the damn contract.

Suddenly furious, she tossed the luggage in the corner of her room, unable to look at it anymore. She pulled out the contract she'd so stupidly signed and read it back to front, multiple times.

There was nothing in there specifically about sex, but it did state "other duties as assigned" multiple times. Did that mean sex? She was supposed to act like his wife on this trip to the Cayman Islands. How much of a honeymooner was she supposed to be?

Tears of frustration leaked out of her eyes, and she brushed them away, pressing into her eyeballs hard, as if she could pry her eyeballs out of her head. She was so damn stupid.

She'd fallen for the rich man with the pretty face.

Like a naïve little girl.

He was probably laughing at her even now.

A knock at the door surprised her. She went to answer, and saw a woman wearing professional attire with a duffel bag slung over her shoulder looking back at her with an expectant smile.

"Can I help you?"

The woman was older, and as she studied her, Amelia realized her professional attire was all stretchy, as if she was prepared to do work. A sudden sinking in her belly almost doubled her over.

"My name is Nancy Schlesinger. Charlie sent me to look after your gram while you go on vacation."

"He did, did he?" Of course he did. He was doing everything. He had said last night he would do this.

All the things Amelia couldn't do for herself, Charlie was doing so she would sleep with him.

Buy her clothes. That didn't work, so he paid her tax bill and paid for a nurse. Her jaw hurt from where she was clenching it so hard, but even as she registered the pain, she also told herself it wasn't this woman's fault.

"Come in." Her own plans were pretty thin. She'd asked the neighbors at the corner to check in on Gram every day, but they were farmers, the people who supplied them with cucumbers for Gram's pickles. They were busy and didn't have the time or energy to look after Amelia's responsibilities. She'd offered to pay them, but it wasn't as much as it was worth to them, probably.

"I take it he didn't tell you?" A knowing smile graced the nurse's lips and Amelia shook her head, chagrined.

"He did, but I didn't realize he was serious. If you'll excuse me, I need to call him really quick. Wait here?"

She walked into her bedroom and slammed the door behind her before calling her boss. Of course, he didn't answer.

She fired off a text message.

> You win on the nurse. But I'm paying you back for that out of my future paychecks. We have to talk about the rest.

Then she sent it off and looked at it, chewing her lip. She decided it wasn't enough.

> I'm not happy about this.

There. That was professional and wouldn't get her fired, but he would know she didn't like it.

On the other hand, what choice did she have with the nurse thing?

Going back out to the living room, she pasted on a smile.

"Okay, let's discuss her routines and your qualifications."

She sighed.

It was a nice chat, and Nancy seemed to like her gram. They were chatting in Gram's room when Amelia went to finish packing. She looked at the mess that was her room, checking her phone to see no new messages. But he had read hers.

This was going to be a long trip.

CHAPTER NINE

The next morning, she chose the least sexy professional clothes she had in her possession. A long flowing skirt and a pair of knee-high boots covered her legs, and a bulky, cowl-necked sweater covered everything else. The day was dreary, so her clothing choice sort of fit the weather. Still, that was just today. As she sat outside and waited for the driver to pick her up, she thought about all the skin that would show this weekend.

She was still angry when Luther picked her up, and angrier still as she answered emails on her phone for Mr. Delmonico on the way to work. He'd insisted she use his driver so she didn't have to make the commute into the city herself. At first, she suspected it was to get more work done, and if that was what he was paying her for, she'd be glad to do it. However, she strongly suspected he was paying for more than her work, so each email she sent only made her angrier.

Pulling up to the curb in front of work, Amelia forced herself to look up at the building she had loved for so long. It looked like the Chrysler building on steroids, taller, wider, and more intimidating. The long, thin windows mirrored the shape of the building, and today reflected the white clouds that covered the sky. The way the windows mirrored the weather so beautifully echoed her mood. It wasn't dark, just finally seeing the cloudy reality of her future.

Luther tipped a hat to her, offering her a kind word for her day, and she took a deep breath and walked inside the lobby. Brooke was sitting at her desk, staring at her. Her mouth was plastered into a fake smile, but her eyes slanted with displeasure.

"Miss Flores, good morning." The words came out through gritted teeth, and Amelia flashed her a genuine smile. The woman's anger only fueled her at this point. It was catty and childish, but Amelia didn't care.

"Good morning," she sing-songed, feeling fake but loving the look on Brooke's face as she sailed by her to go around to the freight elevators.

Freight elevators weren't fancy, and they were bigger than the regular glass elevators. It served to make her feel like she was in an actual room, instead of suspended above the lobby of the building. She was thankful to the delivery guy for showing them to her. It helped bolster herself for the confrontation she knew was coming.

At the office, Mr. Delmonico, as she was forcing herself to refer to him now—not Charlie—was already in his office, shirt sleeves rolled up. Part of her, the stupid part, wished she'd seen him as he got comfortable for his day, as she had fallen for the put-together man in the suit with the cufflinks, and only enjoyed the show as he undressed. But the rational part couldn't stand to look at him in any way, since it only served to remind her why he wanted her to work for him.

So she got busy, confirming the appointments he had today, forwarding him emails, and then scanning documents.

They were leaving for the Cayman Islands this evening, and she was going to have a clean desk when she left.

The phone ringing interrupted her scanning, and she saw him watching her through the windows.

"Delmonico Enterprises, how may I help you?"

"I need an appointment for this morning, please."

"I'm sorry. Mr. Delmonico is full for this morning. All he has today is a three o'clock."

"I don't know if I can get everyone together for three…" The voice on the other end was a man who clearly hadn't expected to not get what he called for. The attitude, so similar to Charlie's … Mr. Delmonico's was exactly what she needed. If she couldn't lash out at him, she would put this client in his place. "Look, we are old friends. I'm sure if you told him Adam Beckett needed an appointment, he would make the time."

She smiled. "I'm in charge of Mr. Delmonico's appointments, and he's booked. He will be out of town next week. Unless you want the week of the sixteenth, you'll get them together for three o'clock today."

"How about we make the appointment, and I'll call if we can't make it." The man was dismissive, as if he were about to hang up.

"Mr. Delmonico's time is valuable, sir, and we don't make appointments on the off chance you show up. If you cancel, you will be charged a cancellation fee, and it's almost triple the rate of actually showing up."

The man sputtered on the other end of the line before acknowledging the terms she had just made up off the top of her head. He didn't make an appointment. She was grinning as she settled the phone back in its cradle, feeling satisfied that she'd managed to get the best of *someone* today.

"Miss Flores, a moment please?" His voice was intense in its quiet. It was a bit scary, but she stood, squared her shoulders, and marched into his office.

His eyes scanned her body, not giving away any reaction. She wondered if he was noticing the unsexiness of her outfit choice today. Amelia quirked an eyebrow and settled a hand at her hip, waiting for him to speak.

"Is your gram okay?"

The topic of conversation threw her. She was expecting something else.

"Um, yeah. She's fine." Her hand fell off her hip, and she clasped them in front of her.

"Everything else fine?" His eyebrows were raised with concern.

"Of course." Not really. She'd just figured out yesterday why she was really here.

Suddenly the concern left his face, and it was filled with something completely different. He stood behind his desk and planted his hands on the top, leaning toward her. She ignored the flex of his forearms with the movement.

"Then please explain to me, *why* you chased off a client?" His voice was a roar, and she flinched, bringing her arms up to her chest. They started knitting together, a nervous habit she had. Amelia tried to stop it, but that would require all her concentration, and he'd just asked her a question.

"Because your time is valuable, sir. They were being wishy-washy with it, and I didn't think they'd actually show up. It was a judgment call, and I made it. If it was the wrong call, I apologize."

"Did they give you a name?" Quieter, he was still angry, but he was watching her hands. She managed to clasp them behind her so if they started clutching at each other, at least he wouldn't see.

"Adam Beckett, sir. He said it was four people and he wasn't sure if they would all be available at three o'clock. I really thought—"

"I don't pay you to think. You have a job that doesn't require much thought at all. You simply do as I ask; do you understand?"

"Other duties as assigned," she muttered, suddenly peeved.

"What?"

"The phrase used to trap me in the contract, sir. Yes, I understand completely." Amelia's voice was rising in pitch, as her entire body vibrated with the restraint of trying not to lose her shit with her boss.

He came around the side of the desk. Leaning on the front, he crossed his arms in front of him, but the gesture was anything but carefree. The tension radiated off him. She could cut the barely controlled restraint with a bread knife if she wanted to.

"You finally read it?" His mouth was a sneer. Still beautiful, but she felt it as it curled around her, covering her with his distaste.

"Yes, I read it. Several times. While you never actually said what you are paying for clearly in the papers, it's plain to me what you are throwing money at me for. The nurse for Gram, my taxes, the sexy clothes, making sure I'm at your beck and call. Utterly dependent on you. I get it. It's what case studies are written for. I can see it."

"Case studies?"

"Manipulators. Abusers."

His face was suddenly washed in shock. "You think I'm abusing you?" Each word that came out of his mouth was increasingly angrier. Her stomach plummeted at his directing it at her, but she stood firm. She wasn't going to back down.

"Isn't that what your job is all about? Manipulation? All you do is manipulate people into doing what you want to make clients happy." The look of angry disbelief on his face made her stop. "You *have* to see what you're doing."

He raked his hand through his hair and let out his breath in a whooshing noise. Finally, he stalked around the desk and dropped into the seat. Looking back up at her, he pierced her with the dark abyss of his eyes.

"That is all. I would offer you lunch, but I'm afraid any act of kindness at this point would be construed as manipulation, so I'll leave you to your own devices."

"Yes, sir." Dismissed, she spun on her heel to retreat to her desk.

He seemed shocked, but expert manipulators were great actors, so she didn't put too much credence in the action.

No matter how genuine he seemed.

CHAPTER TEN

Charlie sat at his desk, staring at Amelia through the glass of his office. He'd been doing this for hours. He couldn't stop himself. She was beautiful in her anger. She was the type of woman who cried when she was mad, and he watched her shoulders rise with every sniffle. He was enraptured by the angry swipes at her face, knowing he wouldn't see tears, but wishing he'd pushed her that much harder so he could.

Except she'd flinched, hadn't she? He wasn't into physically hurting women, unless they wanted it. And while the thought of raising that massive expanse of skirt she wore and spanking her ass until it was red was highly appealing, she had flinched when he'd strode toward her.

She was right. He manipulated people. Killed them when necessary, true.

But he hadn't intended to do that to her. He only wanted to see her more often. He wanted to give her things because she seemed to need them.

He'd had the contract written for months, since the first week she'd started working in the lobby. Her bright smile on her innocent face, surrounded by the dark halo of her sleek bob, all combined to make her a mystery to him. And he liked mysteries.

Yes, there was a shadow behind her eyes, and he wanted to understand it. But he wanted her smiles. Her tears. Her anger. More than the smiles, her anger and her tears were real emotions, not easily faked. He wanted the authentic emotions of someone who so freely gave them.

He had no idea why.

Maybe because he hated it in himself.

Was he manipulating her to get them? Yes, it was possible. He really didn't know any other way.

Truth was, he'd gotten a pitiful amount of work done since she'd started working for him. She was too damn distracting. He imagined her lush little mouth wrapped around his cock every time he watched her purse her lips in concentration. The other night, when she'd drooled on his lap while she slept, the image of her crying and gagging on his dick had almost undone him.

That wasn't even to say the times he took her on top of his desk. In his head, it was a montage of filthy scenes, her bent over, him spanking her, then sinking in. Or she would ride him in his desk chair, his thumb in her asshole. Or him burying his face in her hot, wet pussy while she propped her shoes on his shoulders, again, his thumb in her asshole. He had no idea why he was so fascinated with her ass, but he was going to take it in his fantasies, soon.

Amelia looked up at him, stark anger on her face. The fire in her eyes made his dick jump in his pants, and he reached a hand under his desk to rearrange things.

She dropped her eyes back to her computer screen, ignoring him.

He sighed and pushed his hand through his hair, resting it on the back of his neck and squeezing.

He needed to get control of himself.

Amelia had installed some sort of software on his computer so they could communicate without yelling across the office. He pulled it up and tapped out a message to her.

> I'm not manipulating you.

He deleted it. No sense in opening that can of worms, and he wasn't in the habit of explaining himself. Besides, what would he say? He liked her? No. Charlie Delmonico didn't have feelings like that. Attachments. Sure, he wanted to see her emotions and feelings, but only because he didn't have any of his own.

At three o'clock he watched as the door to the outside opened and in walked Adam and another man, casually striding into the outer office to greet a suddenly flustered Amelia.

The message screen pinged.

Your three o'clock is here. You went around me to make the appointment?

I didn't make it.

She looked at him, and he nodded. She sighed and gestured for them to enter the conference room.

As the men filed around his giant table, he realized what had happened. Mack had a self-satisfied grin on his face, and the new guy clapped him on the back. Charlie remembered he was cyber security, which was a fancy word for a fucking hacker.

He'd gotten into their system and given them the appointment himself.

He was grateful for a distraction.

A distraction from the distraction.

Rising, he strode into the conference room and shut the door. Amelia watched them through the glass, and her frustration was evident. For some reason, he delighted in it. For once, she was as lost as he was.

"She's a ballbuster." The new guy gestured to Amelia and Charlie's hackles immediately rose.

"She can be protective of my time." He was lying. She didn't give a damn about his time. She'd been pissed and took it out on this guy. "You are?"

"I like a woman with some sass. I wish I'd been on the call." The man ignored Charlie's question and grinned wolfishly. Suddenly pissed, Charlie knew exactly where the asshole's mind was. He shot Adam a look, silently wondering how one of his oldest friends thought he could work with this douchebag.

He shook himself. He worked with douchebags every day. Leaning on the table, he got in the asshole's face.

"Miss Flores is not up for discussion. Who the fuck are you?" Charlie gritted his teeth through the change of subject before he lost his shit. If this guy was a hacker, he could use him for other projects; he just needed to figure out how to deal with the guy.

"I'm Mack McKenzie, and I've been doing some work for Adam, here. He's brought it to my attention we have some mutual interests."

"We are taking down Bascom Forrester." Adam, asserting himself as the ringleader, spoke with a certain amount of smugness. "You have others to bring on board?" Looking at Charlie, Adam simply raised an eyebrow.

He didn't have any personal relations with the man, by design. Everyone knew he had his little finger in a lot of pies, some legal, some not so much. He was entirely too visible for Charlie to have anything to do with him.

"I do, but I can't do anything about this for at least a week. I'm in the Caymans next week, wrapping up a few loose ends on a project. After that, I can devote time to this one." Charlie leaned back and steepled his fingers under his chin. This could be interesting. Far more than scaring punks in back alleys and blackmailing city politicians.

"He'll be a hard man to ruin. He's powerful."

"Are you saying you can't do it?" Mack sneered at him. Charlie's patience was running thin. He shot Adam a look, telling him with his eyes to get the guy under control or they'd both be out of here.

"No. I can do most anything. I'm saying it will take a lot of money for the kind of ruin you're talking about."

Mack leaned forward. "I have plans to get money, but we need clean money."

"I can clean the money." Charlie leaned back in his seat. "One of the other guys I was chatting with can too." He pointed to Mack. "You can too, if you're worth your salt as a cybersecurity specialist."

"What do you mean?"

"Let's get together and talk outside of the office. One week. If you've got anything to contribute as far as a specific plan, email it to me. If not, we'll meet at Adam's warehouse next Saturday night. Eight. I'll get the others there. We can all meet." He would give a basic lesson on money laundering. It wasn't hard, if you had the money.

After ushering them out, Charlie sat down at his desk, ignoring the daggers Amelia was shooting at him, and pulled out his phone.

He sent a text to Luca, the owner of the restaurant and Dean, the guy he'd met at the bar, telling them there was a group opportunity, and he needed them to meet at Adam's place next Saturday. He sent them the address, then shut off his phone. If they were serious, they'd fucking show.

Now he just needed to figure out what the fuck to do with the woman who was suddenly pissed at him. And figure out why he cared.

CHAPTER ELEVEN

Amelia had never flown in a private jet before. Truthfully, she hadn't flown anywhere in years. Back when she was younger, she'd had different ideas for her future, and it hadn't been anything to save up for a trip out of state to go see a concert, or something similarly frivolous. But then she'd gotten engaged and all frivolities were over. Then the engagement had ended, so she'd moved in with Gram to lick her wounds. Of course, her grammy was still alive, and when she'd passed, it had been left to her to take care of her great-grandma.

And here she was.

If it weren't for Charlie, she'd be nearly destitute, working the shitty job, about to lose her house, and struggling to take care of the only woman left who loved her.

She leaned back in the plush leather seat, ignoring the man in the seat opposite her, who watched her carefully.

He was her boss. Nothing more.

Never mind his beauty was almost painful to look at sometimes. She just had to remind herself he was using her for sex.

But was he? Or was that her excuse to put him at arm's length?

She looked at him. Yeah, he was still examining her, his eyes raking over her legs now.

They'd changed on the plane before takeoff. She was wearing a short sundress, spaghetti straps, no bra, and a pair of sandals. She felt naked under his gaze.

He, too, had changed into casual island wear. Now he looked like an adult frat boy. His legs were strong, yet lean, in his cargo shorts. The t-shirt he wore stretched across an expanse of muscles she'd never seen on a man, yet she could see clearly defined under his shirt, no doubt as expensive as her designer sandals.

His hair flopped over one eye, an allowance to the casualness of the attire, he hadn't combed it back into its usual neat style. Instead, it gave the illusion he was carefree.

As if he actually took vacations. For some reason, Amelia didn't think he played well at all.

"Why do you think I'm abusing you?" He spoke as if the words left a sour taste in his mouth.

So he'd calmed down now and was going to continue the conversation as if the hours between hadn't happened? Fine.

"Manipulating me, not abusing." She took a deep breath and forged on. "For sex. You're paying for all these things for me to have sex with you. It would go right along with our honeymoon thing." She stated the words in as matter-of-fact a tone as she could muster, but honestly, the words sounded stupid out loud.

"It's rather expensive, don't you think?" He was smiling at her. *Now* he was laughing at her. "I could have any number of women without nearly half the trouble."

"Then why spend all this money on me?"

He sighed and leaned back in his seat, mirroring her pose. His legs stretched out, and he planted his canvas boat shoes between her sandals.

"Because I don't want someone in my employ going without. I simply paid for things you needed. It's what I do." He paused, still studying her. "I'll admit to an attraction to you, but you may have read it as more. I'm planning on staying professional, and *professionally* sometimes, I need a date, or a wife."

"But I've read some of your files. You use blackmail to get what you want in return. I'm not a fool."

"If you've read my files, you also know that I make people disappear as well." His words were deadly, and a shiver rippled across her skin. Was she taunting a demon? Why would he say that to her?

She didn't say anything to that, simply looked out the window into the darkness. It was encompassing, inky. As if it were a void.

She felt like that sometimes. Like she was just a black hole, waiting to swallow everything around her into the nothingness that she was. Like now, she was disappearing. If she didn't come back from this trip, no one would know where she went. Her gram wouldn't even realize she'd ever been, much less that she was gone.

Was that what people were? Their only consciousness was other people's feelings for them? Since her gram didn't know she existed as herself, thinking she was some grand-niece from Regency England, and not Amelia, did Amelia Flores even exist?

"No need to make me disappear, Mr. Delmonico," she whispered.

"As if I could." His eyes were on hers, intense and needy. It made her warm, and a trickle of sweat ran between her shoulder blades. She pressed against the seat, squashing it into her dress. "Sleep. We still have a couple of hours before we get there."

**

Apparently, Amelia slept like the dead, because she awoke in a luxuriously soft bed with sunlight streaming into her eyes. She jackknifed up, awareness hitting her at once. She was still wearing her dress from the night before, but she had absolutely no memory beyond the airplane.

Charlie was lying next to her, and he chuckled at her actions. As intimate as the moment was, she felt a quiver of fear tremble through her bones. Their last conversation had been about her disappearing, hadn't it?

Yet here he was *chuckling* at her. It was almost a foreign sound from the normally put-together man, so stoic and powerful. The chuckle was almost roguish and reminded her of a wolf disguised as a sheep to tempt innocents.

She threw the comforter off herself and swung her legs over the side of the bed, needing to sit up and have some space between them. They were in bed together, and she had no idea what had happened.

"You slept like the dead. I did my obligatory duty and carried you over the threshold, joking with the bellman that we would have to do it again, when you were conscious. If I didn't know any better, I'd think you were drugged. You sleep hard."

She did sleep hard. Everyone had always joked that if she slept during a tornado, she'd be carried off to the land of Oz.

But she'd never slept through something like this. A plane ride, presumably a car ride to the hotel, and then the check-in and being carried Lord knew how far.

It was disconcerting, waking up in such different circumstances as when she'd fallen asleep. She could have been drugged. She turned her head to look at Charlie.

Lying in bed, sheets around his hips, he reclined against the pillows and headboard, his chest naked.

And freaking glorious.

She'd imagined him without a shirt, multiple times. He filled out his suits and shirts like a man who saw a gym regularly, but her imagination didn't do reality justice. He was chiseled from granite, hard planes of sinewy muscle covered with golden skin and the dark hair of a man. His chest was awe-inspiring and the hair tapered into a trail on his belly, disappearing under the sheets in a way that had her mouth suddenly watering like a woman starved.

She swallowed and turned her head back to the front.

A magnificent view of the Caribbean ocean greeted her. Now that she was a bit calmer, she realized the sliding glass door was open and she could hear the waves crashing into the shoreline. She stood and walked to where she could see better.

"I've never seen an ocean. I mean, we live on a bay, but I've never been anywhere there's this much water," she mused quietly. "So blue..." She could hear the rustle of sheets as Charlie stood, and she risked a glance behind her.

He was standing at the closet, naked as the day he was born.

She inhaled swiftly and turned back to the ocean view, the image of his naked rear burned into her brain. The godlike chiseling extended to his backside, where she had never seen a man with the sort of musculature she saw in her boss.

His ass was firm, and his legs powerful. Amelia had no idea what use those muscles on his back would be for, but she imagined exploring the bumps and ridges with her tongue.

"What's our plan today?" Her voice was strangled, and she cleared her throat to start over. "What are we supposed to do?"

She heard him dragging clothes up his legs and tried again to face him. He was tugging a t-shirt over his head, his rumpled hair popping out of the neck hole.

"We are honeymooners, so I think since the banks are closed, we should practice acting like that while we explore things. I can book us a scuba tour?"

She shuddered. "No, thank you. I saw *Open Water* and it send scuba diving to the bottom of my bucket list."

He shrugged as he bent to put on his shoes. "Parasailing?"

"*Jurassic Park*. The second one."

Shoes on, he straightened. "What would you like to do?"

She looked over her shoulder at the aqua blue water, the likes of which she'd never imagined she'd see in her lifetime.

"Can we just go to the beach?"

Charlie smiled at her, and it was absolutely glorious. It lit his dark face like nothing she'd ever seen before and gave her a warmth in her chest. She smiled back at him.

"I'll order us some breakfast and have a picnic lunch prepared. You take the first shower and we'll go after we eat." He was still in control, the all-powerful-killer-Charlie-with-a-plan. But he was smiling, and she liked it.

CHAPTER TWELVE

Amelia found her impatience building as she waited for room service, while Charlie showered and got ready for his day. She changed into her bathing suit and packed a bag for the beach, hoping she anticipated everything she would need. A towel, sunscreen, a book to read, her phone, an extra pair of shoes, a dress to wear in case they decided to do something different, was all neatly folded and arranged as their breakfast arrived.

She answered the door and oohed and aahed at the arrangement of exotic fruit and cheeses, an enormous omelet, eggs Benedict, and a plate full of bacon was artfully arranged on a wheeled table in the living room. Amelia searched through her purse, wondering how much was appropriate to tip the man who'd brought the food, when he waved her off.

"No worries. It's taken care of. Please let me know if you need anything, Mrs. Stryker."

Charlie chose that moment to come out of the bathroom, dressed in nothing but a towel wrapped around his waist. He strode over to Amelia and wrapped his arm around her waist from behind before dropping a kiss onto her shoulder. The shock at his touch and hot mouth on her cooled skin had her stiffening.

"Thank you very much." He spoke to the man, who winked and smiled.

"I'll leave the honeymooners to it, then," he said as he let himself out.

The arm dropped from around her and the heat of him left her backside. "You need to relax and pretend you like me for this trip, or you don't have much use."

Then he went back into the bedroom to dress.

He was right. She did need to relax. One of the reasons he'd hired her was to pose as his wife for whatever covert dealings he had. Amelia didn't need to know and didn't want to think about what his end goal was, only that she was necessary.

They were on their honeymoon. She could do what was necessary.

After her little pep talk, she sat down to eat. Charlie came out and sat opposite her.

"I'm sorry. I guess I'm a little off-balance still, waking up someplace so different. I know what my job is; I'll do better." She managed to flash him a smile before digging into the fruit plate and loading her own plate with an assortment of mangoes and some other fruit she wasn't familiar with. She also put some cheese on her plate, and Charlie dished her over half of the eggs Benedict, as well as half of the omelet. She grabbed her own bacon.

"I understand." He didn't sound like he did, but his words helped. "I'm not used to this either. I've always hired an escort from a service, and they're more skilled at acting, because they're paid to be. And they certainly don't argue with me about things." She ignored the twinge of jealousy at the image of other women with Charlie Delmonico. She was a big girl. This was a no-sex situation, right? He was saying so right now. So why did the idea of him having sex with other women in the past affect her like this? "This is a different situation entirely."

"The difference being, escorts have sex with you to make the charade more believable?"

To her surprise, his eyes hardened and he settled his silverware across his own plate before leveling a stern gaze on her. She swallowed the piece of foreign fruit she'd just put in her mouth, its initial sweet taste turning sour in her stomach.

What had she said?

"They do things to make the charade more believable, yes. We kiss, touch each other, and murmur in each other's ears. They act like lovers. They don't stiffen up when I touch them. They melt into my embrace. Then, yes, we do fuck." He grabbed his fork between elegant fingers and speared a bite of omelet. "But then again, they don't know I'm a killer."

He spoke low, his voice caressing her skin, causing goosebumps to break out.

He'd actually said the words out loud. He was a killer. That should affect her in some way, but instead, she found herself reacting to his other words.

Despite her misgivings about his job, Amelia found herself crossing her legs under the table, trying to alleviate the throbbing ache his words evoked. She was suddenly hot, and the throbbing inside her was deliciously uncomfortable.

She wanted all of those things.

Especially the part about not knowing he was a killer.

If she didn't know that, would she be willing to do the rest?

"I can do most of that, Mr. Delmonico."

"It's Charlie. And not Delmonico. It's—"

"Stryker. Yes. I'm Mrs. Stryker," she finished for him, letting him know she was on board.

"And how much are you willing to do?"

She swallowed. "Kiss. Melt. All of the things besides the sex."

His eyes darkened, and she wondered how far he was going to go. He looked at her like she'd just challenged him and he was going to make her regret it.

And then, when they were back home, in the city, at work, how in the hell she was going to forget his lips on hers and actually get work done?

**

Amelia's bathing suit was going to be the death of him, even with what passed as a cover-up. It was mesh and completely see-through, so he could see every exposed curve. She'd avoided turning her back to him, but he'd seen it when he'd come out of the bathroom, and she'd been talking to the hotel boy who'd brought breakfast.

He'd nearly groaned at the sight. He could kiss whoever told her this was a suit he would like, because he was confident Amelia wouldn't have it otherwise.

It was a string bikini, not rare at all, but the butt of it went deep into her crack, showing off the ass he'd imagined so many times. A deep purple, her tits spilled around the edges of the triangles, which was heavenly enough. But the bottoms were fucking exquisite.

He longed to walk behind her with the dual advantages of getting to see her walk in it, her ass bouncing with each step, and blocking anyone else's view of her. But he settled with walking next to her, draping an arm around her waist, tugging her next to him. She looked up at him, her eyes so wide and innocent he wanted to get lost in them. She wrapped her arm around his waist, clinging to him. Then offered him a small smile.

Charlie liked it more than he cared to admit. She had said she was willing to do the things his escorts did, so he dropped his mouth to hers, taking what she was inadvertently offering him.

As soon as his lips touched hers, in what was supposed to be a casual peck on the lips, she froze again. He stopped walking and wrapped the arm around her waist tighter, tugging her to his body, willing her to melt.

Melt, dammit.

And melt, she did. Her soft curves molded to him, her pelvis against his, her breasts pressing against him. Her mouth opened, and he took it, like a pirate and his plunder.

He dropped the picnic basket the hotel had packed and wrapped his other hand around her, grabbing the ass he'd fantasized about. Firm, supple, Jesus God, it was everything he wanted.

And her tongue was so sweet as it timidly touched his own. They swirled together in an exploratory dance that had him hard as a goddamn rock. He broke the kiss before he lost control and stared at her breathlessly.

He was still grabbing her ass, his hand having delved between the cheeks into the heat he craved.

She breathed every bit as hard as he did, her tits pressed against his bare chest, her nipples poking him through her suit.

"Shit. Just like that." His voice didn't sound normal, but that was expected. She had just kissed him better than any other of the women he'd paid for the experience had. He forced himself to take a step back and adjusted his erection in his suit before stooping to pick up the picnic basket and dropping his arm back over her shoulders. "Just fucking like that."

That was all he could manage to say as he led them to two lounge chairs on the beach. He scooted them together, as newlyweds would. That's what he told himself anyway, because he didn't want a doubt in any other man's mind that she wasn't his. They weren't siblings on some family vacation together. They were fucking *together*.

She didn't speak as she settled into the lounge chair and got out some sort of lotion and started spreading it across her smooth skin. He watched, unable not to, and realized he was so goddamn hungry for her. It would be a miracle if he made it through this week without fucking her the way he wanted.

Needed.

Yeah, she was a distraction he could hardly afford, since he hadn't thought of anything else since he'd awoken to find her sleeping next to him. She was so damn sweet and innocent, and he'd just watched her, marveling at how she'd ended up in his bed. Amelia had been angry yesterday. It was a familiar anger, born of fear, and he fucking loved it.

He had a great desire to see more of it. He loved it when people were afraid of him; it gave him power, and he wanted power over Amelia.

Now, she wasn't afraid of him, but she *wanted* him. That much was obvious, from the way she'd clenched at their talk over breakfast, to her agreement to do some physical things with him, to the kiss they'd just shared.

And he loved that too. He had a desire to see how far she would go with that want.

As she caressed her skin, rubbing sunscreen into it, he realized her skin was delicate, unkissed by the sun. She would burn if she didn't use it.

"Turn over, let me." He wasn't capable of complete sentences at this point, but she understood what he wanted.

Starting at her shoulders, he smoothed the lotion over her skin, then rubbed it in. Then he moved down her back, making sure to get underneath the string that tied, resisting the urge to untie it. Then down her back, to her ass. He spent a lot of time there, rubbing and smoothing, pulling her cheeks apart to see what he could see. The valley to her pussy had him groaning aloud, and he didn't give a shit who heard him.

He massaged her as he rubbed in the lotion, going back over her again, spending even more time on the delicate cheeks of her ass. He didn't want her skin to burn, certainly not there. He wanted to spread her wide and fuck her there. Badly.

She was his. He wasn't pretending now. As he rubbed the lotion down the backs of her legs, he was lost in the feel of her smooth skin, the way it lightened when he pressed down, then reddened slightly in his wake. He wondered how it would look with the blush of a good spanking, and he was hard again.

Then he kissed the back of her calves, the backs of her knees, watching the goosebumps on her skin. The breeze off the ocean cooled the sun, but her skin was downright hot as he kissed, then nipped at the globes of her ass before kissing again, first one then the other. He licked up her back, tasting salt and sunscreen as he got to her shoulders, where he kissed her again. She whimpered and squirmed slightly, but didn't move.

When he finished, he went back to his own chaise lounge, and reclined, watching her. She stayed where she was, on her stomach, with her eyes closed. He looked at the press of her tits on the chair, admiring the curves.

Finally, he forced himself to lean back in the chair and close his eyes, lurid images of the two of them together burning his retinas.

**

Amelia didn't know which way was up by the time Charlie had finished with her body. When he'd started, she been so tense she didn't know how she would ever relax. By the time he was done, she was putty, nothing but a dripping puddle of sensations on the beach.

He'd taken his time, inviting all sorts of images of sensual lovemaking, sweaty nights on rumpled sheets, cries of ecstasy in the darkened air of their hotel room. His hands were large, rough, and entirely welcome. He could do what he wanted to and she'd be on board with all of it, no matter what she had told him over breakfast.

When he was finished, she dozed, until a trickle of sweat ran down her leg and she decided to walk to the water to cool off.

"I'm going to go dip in the water and get wet."

Charlie wore sunglasses, so she couldn't see his eyes, but he told her, "I'll watch." The tone of his voice suggested more, but she wasn't sure how to take it, so she simply gave him a small smile before getting up.

She walked down to the water, aware of his eyes on her. She didn't like this bathing suit. It wasn't comfortable at all, but he made her feel really pretty when he looked at her in it, so maybe it wasn't all that bad. The part she hated the most, he seemed to really enjoy if the amount of time he'd spent rubbing sunscreen into her bottom was any indication.

She sighed, wondering what she'd gotten herself into with him. She was attached, as much as she didn't want to be. Amelia longed for things to happen between them, even though she was scared of the man, and didn't know how to act when they got back to work.

She got into the water up to her thighs and looked down. She could see her toes, with little silvery fishes swimming around them, darting this way and that. A few swam up and nibbled, testing her out, before dashing away. It tickled, and she giggled, shifting her feet to watch them scatter.

Pulling water up her body with her hands, she felt the coolness as it cascaded over her body, then went a little deeper before turning back to the shore. Charlie was on the chair, his sunglasses-clad eyes on her. She gave him a little wave, then dove into the water.

It was cool, but not cold, and she felt it against her heated face as she swam a little ways underwater before coming back up. She brushed her hair back off her face and paddled around a little before declaring herself cool and going back. She'd get some sun on her front side while she read her book.

When she returned, Charlie held two glasses of something bright yellow with tiny umbrellas and skewers of fruit sticking out of the top.

She decided right then and there to just go with things. Charlie Delmonico couldn't be all that bad, and this was a vacation she'd never ever dreamed of going on. She would enjoy it and do what he was paying her to do. After that rubdown, even sex wasn't off the table, if he wanted.

CHAPTER THIRTEEN

They spent the next two days playing at being honeymooners in the sunshine. She kissed him whenever she got the chance and let him rub sunscreen on her backside when he told her that's what he was going to do. Charlie didn't ask. Ever. And she didn't mind.

They snorkeled, and she couldn't get over all the fish that just swam around them, seemingly unafraid. The underwater landscape was breathtaking, and she spent a long time just floating and looking, everything quiet in the oasis under water.

They sat on the beach and drank fruity drinks, and ate the picnic lunches the hotel staff packed. It was decadent, and Amelia didn't have any problems pretending she was rich and used to this sort of lifestyle.

It was fun.

And she spent the entire time on the edge of going mad with arousal as he couldn't seem to keep his hands off her. He liked her second bathing suit even more than the first, apparently. It was similar to the first, only instead of deep purple, it was white with small pink flowers on it, and had a small ruffle along her hip before delving into the depths of her butt. She was getting used to his ogling her down there, even giving him a little shimmy when she first emerged from the bathroom wearing it.

Monday morning, they woke to shower and dress like real people instead of beach bums. They had an appointment to open an account that afternoon.

He wore a light-gray suit, and she dressed in a tight-fitting dress that opened up and flowed below her knees. It was demure enough for a bank setting, yet sexy enough for the island life she was falling in love with. It had wide straps over her shoulders, and a squared neckline that dipped low enough to show her tanning cleavage. The time in the sunshine had given her pale skin the kiss of the sun, and she felt beautiful on Charlie's arm.

She slicked her dark hair back from her face, letting it fall behind her ears, and wore little diamond studs from her grandma.

"Wear heels."

She tilted her head and complied, finding a pair of silver heels with straps around the ankles and putting them on.

She didn't question him, because she now looked perfect.

As they walked out of the lobby, her hand on his arm, he leaned down to her ear. "You look gorgeous."

She beamed up at him and gave him a peck on the lips, ignoring how very *not pretend* it felt. "I feel gorgeous."

"I can tell." His other hand came on top of hers and gave it a squeeze. She wondered if any of this was an act for him, then shut down that thought. She knew what was happening, and she couldn't afford for it to. She was developing feelings for this man, and she knew it was because he'd basically paid for her to have a new life, and here she was, turning into everything she'd promised herself she wouldn't. Then she'd talked herself around it, justifying her own actions.

She was liking this pretend life he'd paid for.

No better than one of his escorts.

That thought soured her mood.

"I booked us a couples massage after the bank, to keep up with appearances."

"Okay," she said, even though the idea of him spending more money on her turned her stomach. Everything was fine as long as they were on the beach, but now he was back to business Charlie, and she was his arm candy. Exactly what he'd told her in the "interview" when he'd hired her.

She'd do well to remember.

"And I wanted to warn you, there will be an exorbitant amount of money exchanged today. Don't act shocked. Mr. Stryker is a day trader and doesn't want to pay taxes on the amount of money he's acquired."

"Gotcha."

It was all a ruse. Every bit of it.

But he was so good at it. When they arrived at the bank, he helped her out of the car with an outstretched hand, and immediately wrapped his arm around her waist and walked her inside.

"Mr. and Mrs. Stryker! So happy you could break away from paradise to meet with us. I'm Anthony Wright." A well-dressed gentleman with dark hair and skinny mustache met them at the door. How he knew their name was a mystery, but Charlie shook his hand warmly.

"It's a pleasure to be here. This is a beautiful island, and we are enjoying ourselves immensely. Aren't we, darling?" He looked down at her for an answer, his eyes twinkling with the shared game.

"Yes, so much! I'm wanting to do a boat tour later in the week. Do you have any you'd recommend?"

"Absolutely," the rich island accent made Amelia feel welcomed and warm. She really could live here. "I have several private charters I can recommend. Let's go into my office and get the business out of the way."

Charlie had a large duffel bag, and presumably it held cash, that he carried in the hand he wasn't using to hold Amelia. When they followed Mr. Wright into his office, Charlie took her hand in his.

They sat, and while the men talked, Amelia's mind wandered. She looked at Charlie's square jaw and lush lips as he spoke. He shaved off the stubble of the weekend this morning, and she'd almost missed it. Not that she'd ever touched it, but she had imagined what it might feel like. And it had felt nice when they kissed.

She wanted to kiss him more. Even if this was a ruse. She'd gotten back into the justification of things and knew that's where she wanted to stay for the duration of the holiday. She could get back to the self-loathing when they got home.

"How much are we depositing today?" Mr. Wright asked pleasantly, but the greedy glimmer to his eyes couldn't be mistaken.

Charlie casually spouted a number, and aside from a brief widening of her eyes, Amelia was proud of her reaction.

That much money fit into the duffel? And they'd had it with them this entire time? Left in their room? Granted, she watched him get it out of the room safe this morning, but still. That was a monumental shit ton of money.

**

Back at the hotel, their business at the bank concluded, Charlie took her hand and led her straight to the spa.

"I sure could use something to relax after that." He murmured as they went to where a man dressed in scrubs greeted them.

"Mr. and Mrs. Stryker, come this way."

He led them to a room with two massage tables. "Undress and cover with the sheet. We will be back in a moment."

Amelia was a bit surprised to see Charlie shedding his clothing almost immediately. When he dropped his boxers, she realized the masseuse meant all the way nude. She averted her eyes and turned around to undress herself.

"Come on … Don't deprave me," he was wheedling, and Amelia spent a moment relishing the thought that Charlie Delmonico was almost begging her for something. Then she gave in.

She turned and lifted her dress, revealing a bra and thong set. She reached around to unclasp her bra and it fell to the floor before she bent to retrieve it and her dress and put them in a chair.

"Leave the thong on," he growled at her from his spot on his table, erection proudly jutting up to reach skyward.

She did as he commanded, and slipped under the sheet, using it to cover her breasts. Charlie had covered himself as well, and was currently cupping his cock, squeezing it tightly, while he stared at the ceiling.

"Christ, Amelia," he began. "Your body is fantastic." He looked like he was going to say more, but a soft knock at the door interrupted him, and a man and woman came in wheeling a tray of heated stones, towels, and various oils.

The woman rubbed on Amelia while the man worked on Charlie. It didn't take long for her to succumb to the skilled touch of the woman. She was completely relaxed and almost asleep by the time she finished and left her alone with Charlie.

Her mind was wandering around all the sex they could have. Him kissing her neck, her shoulders, her chest. Her breasts, he would pay special attention to, laving them with his warm tongue. Then he would go lower…

"You ready to go back to the room?" His voice, husky with his own relaxation, broke into her reverie. At some point in the massage, she'd rolled over, and now she found herself pressing her pubic bone into the table, unfulfilled desire pulsing through her.

"Actually …" She was so relaxed, she should stop talking and just nod, but she couldn't. "I was thinking sex might not be off the table."

Had she really just said that out loud?

A muttered curse met her ears, and her eyes snapped open. He stared at her, disbelief etched in his strong features. He was sitting on the edge of his own table, reaching for his trousers. He tugged them on and grabbed at his shirt, shrugging it on, before wrapping his underwear in his jacket and reaching for her things.

He tossed the dress at her and stuffed her bra in his pants pocket. "Let's go, then."

CHAPTER FOURTEEN

Charlie could hardly believe it. He hadn't had it this bad for a woman ever, and he'd promised himself he wouldn't fucking touch her beyond what she'd promised him. In spite of the fact his fantasies had him fucking ruining her, he'd been the perfect gentleman.

But she'd given him the green light, and here he was, in the wrong damn place for all the filthy fantasies he'd had.

He hustled her out of the spa area of the hotel, and decided to take advantage of the beachfront, taking her around the outside. There was a party on the beach, tiki torches, portable bars, a giant fire, and people everywhere.

But not by their room.

He stopped her outside the sliding glass door and pushed her against the wall, holding her face in his hands.

"Are you sure this is what you want?" He hated how needy he sounded, but if she stopped him as soon as he lost control, he wasn't sure he could stop.

She stared at him with those deep fathomless eyes of hers and licked her lips before nodding.

He kissed her then, aware of the group of people fifty yards behind him and not giving a shit. Every other kiss before this one had been for show, for the people watching. Now, as he was sure no one was really watching them, he wanted them to. He wanted them to see she was giving herself to him.

She was his.

Using his hands, he pressed her mouth to his in a punishing kiss, demanding apology. She'd been so beautiful, so untouchable, and she would regret that he'd had to wait so long to taste her without pretense.

She moaned, and he used the desire to ramp her up more. He was about to burst, but he would take his. Eventually. For now, he would show her what she'd been missing by holding out.

He kissed down her neck, sucking and nibbling until he got to her shoulders. Removing one strap, he realized the fabric of the dress was stretchy, and he tugged it down to free a breast.

Which he practically mauled. Amelia's sweet hands had found his hair and tangled in it, pressing him closer. She was leaning on the wall, her shoulders supporting her, while she arched into him. He reached for the hem of her dress, tugging it up and wrapping one leg around him as he delved into the darkness under her dress.

She was gasping his name.

"Feel it, Amelia. Feel what you do to me." He thrust his erection into the juncture between her thighs, letting the hard ridge of his cock do his talking. She moaned as she rubbed against it, and he replaced it with a hand, teasing the fabric of her white thong aside and finding her needy, wet heat.

It didn't take much. His kisses, one hand tweaking the nipple of her breast, and the other buried in her sweet pussy, before she fell apart on a cry, yelling his name into the darkness.

Where the partygoers surely knew she belonged to him now.

He kissed her once again, breathing hard, as he straightened her dress. Whispering against her lips, he told her the things he wanted to do to her.

"You have no idea. I want to spank that ass, while I twist your hair between my fingers and pull. Choking. I'm going to rip that ass in two." He had to breathe deeply to form a complete sentence, this woman messed with him so badly. "I'll fuck you so rough you will be ruined for anyone else but me. Me, Amelia. You're mine."

It was like a switch flipped, and she stiffened. Her trembling legs no long shook, and her eyes weren't dazed with lust anymore. Disgust filled her eyes now, and he took a step back to see her fully.

She pushed him the rest of the way and ran inside.

No fucking way was she stopping this.

He followed her in, slamming the door behind him.

"What the fuck?" He should have known. She was a goddamn prick tease. He'd seen it in her naiveté. He should have known she'd balk at him.

"I don't want you to hurt me. I've been there, done that, thank you. Not interested."

"I don't want to marry you. I want to fuck you. Jesus. Do you do this with every man you fuck? It's a fuck!"

She flinched every time he said the word, and he relished it. *"Fuck! Fuck!"* She was shaking again, but it was anger. Her face was red, but not with the blotchy haze of desire. She was pissed at him, and he just kept going, he couldn't stop. "I don't want to marry my fucking secretary. I want to fuck her. Maybe a blowjob. This doesn't mean hearts and flowers. Are you so stupid you thought it did?"

Now she was crying. He wanted to lick the tears and knew as soon as he thought it, it was wrong, but it was an urge he had anyway.

"No, I didn't think it meant hearts and flowers, Charlie." She spoke through her tears, and it was one of the most heartbreakingly beautiful things he'd ever heard. His dick was still hard, throbbing against his zipper, begging for a release. "But I won't let you hurt me."

Realization hit him. She didn't mean the emotional hurt. Maybe this was salvageable.

He ran his hand through his hair and tried to figure out how to fix this, even as he realized he'd never had to work so hard to get a woman into his bed in his life. Was she worth it?

He thought about how tight her pussy was with just a finger, and realized he needed his dick in that. He thought of the birth control pills on the bathroom counter and imagined going in bare.

Fuck.

Yes. She was worth it.

"Okay. Sit." She did, automatically. Her knees folded and she landed on the edge of the bed. "Take off your clothes." He just needed a little more finesse than he'd shown earlier. When he'd been talking, he told her of fantasies he had, but he realized she wasn't the type of woman to go there without a little warming up. He knew that; he had just forgotten in the heat of the moment.

She sat there, not taking off the dress, so he sat next to her and peeled one strap off one shoulder.

"Pleasure and pain go together for me. I've always liked sex a little rough." He kissed her shoulder, then sucked on the skin. Then he bit it gently, and she flinched before he licked where he'd bitten her. He tasted the oil from the massage, but she started shivering.

"I have never made love to a woman, not since I was too young to know what anything meant." Slowly, he inched the other sleeve off of her with his other hand and tugged her dress down to expose both breasts.

"Your tears are exquisite, Amelia." He gave in then and licked her face, tasting the salty tracks of her tears with a groan, even as he squeezed a nipple before testing the weight of her breasts in his palms. "Fucking beautiful." He leaned back and watched her. She still sat up, rigid, but she wasn't shaking anymore, and she watched him carefully to see what he would do next. His girl was even leaning toward him, slightly.

"I long to see my handprints on you, red where I've marked you in passion. A passion born from desire, Amelia, not pain to hurt. Pain to pleasure." He dipped his head to her breast and engulfed it with his mouth. She arched into him, and he pulled back, sucking on the nipple only. Hard. She hissed in air.

"Feel what that does to your pussy? It's clenching and wet, isn't it?" He looked up at her, and she nodded at him. "Your body knows." He went back to mouthing her breast, tugging and pulling with suction, then biting softly on the nipple, letting go to suck his teeth against it. "See? Pleasure and pain. The slight bit of pain heightens the pleasure."

He had no idea what sort of nonsense he was spilling at her, but she seemed to be eating it up.

"For future reference, I like pain too. Scrape your teeth up my dick when you're blowing me, sink your fingernails into my skin, scratch them down my back while I'm fucking you. All of it. More. I love it."

"Oh God," she whispered.

"Yes. Now lean back and let me fuck you, Amelia."

As if he'd lit a fire under her ass, she scooted up the bed, pulling off her dress as she went. She started undoing the straps of her sandals, but he stopped her.

"No. Dig those heels into my ass while I'm fucking you." Standing, he shed his clothing, eyeing her the entire time. She timidly took off her panties, and he was rewarded with a wet spot in the crotch of them.

Fucking gorgeous.

He lowered himself over her, then moved down, sucking and biting as he went, until he got to her pussy. Lifting her legs over his shoulders, she did, in fact, rest the sharp heels on his back, and the scratching of them on his skin had a rumble of awareness moving sharply up his spine.

And then he dipped his head and tasted her.

**

Amelia had gone into this with a certain amount of trepidation, but so far, he hadn't really hurt her. His words outside had scared her, sure. Especially when pictures of Jackson hitting her and using her hair to drag her around the house so he could hit her some more filled her mind. But Charlie had only caused a minimal amount of pain and it was in tandem with some serious pleasure, so she was intrigued.

When he latched his mouth on her clit and started sucking hard, all thoughts of Jackson fled. As they should. Charlie's mouth seemed to fit over her nether regions in just the perfect way, the suction of his mouth so intense, she nearly screamed as she dug into the sheets with her fingernails to find some tether to reality.

Her thighs shook, and she pressed her feet down, indeed digging the heels of these shoes into his back, trying to find some purchase somewhere. Charlie made a noise she could only take as approval, and she remembered how he'd told her to dig into his back. He liked it. The warmth his noise sent into her pussy was yet one more sensation for her to register.

But she was too busy flying. It was almost like an out-of-body experience. The sensations of him were everywhere. One hand twisting her nipple, while the other wrapped around her thigh, keeping her spread for him, even while she was squeezing them closed against the torturous pleasure.

It hurt. It was delicious.

Her hands started stroking his hair, gripping it, then stroking again.

Charlie unwrapped his hand and delved fingers inside her. The sloppy noises of her wetness as he sloshed in and out of her should have been embarrassing, but instead they added to the eroticism of the experience. She wasn't Amelia Flores. She was something else. She was wanted, lusted after, and being pleasured out of her mind.

Charlie used his teeth on her now; his sharp incisors pinched her flesh, scraping against it, while his fingers spread and scissored inside her. Then something foreign started happening—a stinging sensation down there in a place she'd never felt it before.

Somehow, he was pushing a finger inside her rear. It was an invasion, and she couldn't stop it. Her pelvis came off the bed to writhe away from him, as she tugged on his hair to pull him up, but he twisted her nipple painfully in response, shoving the digit in deeper, and she succumbed to the darkest pleasure she'd ever imagined.

Charlie made a noise into her, his teeth replaced by a flicking tongue, and the pleasure turned to a white-hot inferno of carnality. She was pushing herself into his mouth; his fingers were pulsing in and out of her holes, and she felt so full and wanton and needing more, but it was all too much. She was about to die, and she needed more.

Then she was a quivering mass of sensations in the bed, while he was kissing the inside of her thighs, and rising from his perch between her legs. He shoved his pants down his legs, and removing his shirt, and she could only stare, rendered mute by the sight and what he'd done to her.

His eyes were darker than they'd been, and his shoulders quivered with restraint. Charlie's hands went to her hips, and he flipped her over, tugging her into a kneeling position, one hand on her shoulders to keep them down.

Then he plunged inside her, stretching her already sore tissue. Again and again, each thrust taking her breath away. His hands on her ass, spreading it. Then only one hand. When his other hand returned, he pressed something against the tight ring of muscle.

"No," she pleaded. Once had been enough, but she'd been mindless with pleasure. Now it had gone, and he was riding her, sticking what had to be his thumb inside her. "It hurts."

"Only for a moment. You'll stretch." His voice was ragged and he ignored her plea.

He was right though. As he moved inside her, stroking places in her depths, she did, in fact, stretch to accommodate him. The initial burn gave way to simply pressure, and he pushed on something inside her, until she was climbing that terrifying, painful precipice again.

He leaned over her, biting her shoulder as his other hand went around to rub at her clit. He was balancing on an elbow, to keep the totality of his weight off her, and as he rubbed and pinched, his tongue was doing things to her neck and shoulder and in that moment, Amelia had the impression that she was taken care of, that her pleasure was important. Necessary.

That's when she fell apart again. She tried not to think about the thumb in her asshole, but rather the cock inside her and the fingers on her nub and the mouth on her neck, but at his grunts of release, the twitching of him inside her, the hot jets of his release against her inner walls, she began contracting her orgasm once more.

She cried out and fell forward, unable to take any more from him.

Charlie lay on his side next to her, breathing heavily, and used one arm to tug her into a spoon. He shushed her, making soothing noises in her ear, calling her beautiful.

That's when she realized she was crying.

CHAPTER FIFTEEN

The rest of their time in the Cayman Islands passed in a blur of pleasure and pain, sunshine and salty water. They drank fruity drinks on the beach, took a tour of the sea around them, saw dolphins and sharks, and schools of colorful fish. He put sunscreen on her body, especially her rear end, toying with the tight puckered hole he was so fond of, and gave her more than one climax on the white sands of the beach.

He'd devoted the remaining time there to showing Amelia his distinctive brand of enjoyment, and instead of giving her a sense of peace, it only served to make her more conflicted.

What would happen when they got back to the States and he resumed his job? Would she still only be his secretary? Or would she be more?

Sitting on the sand, she was glad for her sunglasses so he couldn't see her eyes. The word girlfriend didn't apply to a man like Charlie. He'd said as much when he'd thought she was angling for a relationship with him. He didn't do hearts and flowers, and she'd do well to remember that.

At night, the orgasms he gave her brought tears to her eyes, and he'd lick them off, muttering words about how beautiful she was in her pain.

The pain wasn't anything she'd ever experienced before. It was the complete darkness of a hurricane, just before the beauty of the storm that left devastation in its path.

It was the devastation of impending death, before the beauty of peace.

It was everything.

And nothing. Because she didn't have a word to pin to it. Like her own existence. Did she only exist as Charlie's secretary? His secret lover? It was like Gram, only knowing her as a pretend ward, coming in at night after a day out, where Gram imagined she went on social calls and outings with friends, as ladies of leisure in eighteenth century society did. But Gram didn't *know* her. And neither did Charlie. Not really. But he seemed to know her body, and this week, that was all that really mattered, wasn't it?

Sometimes it seemed she was pretending for all of it, except the times with Charlie, where her pleasure pain was his chief goal.

"You need more sunscreen on your back." His words were enough on the surface, but she heard the underlying desire. Their beach was relatively private, owned by the hotel, and at the moment was nearly empty. The only people on it were a hundred yards away.

She smiled at him, wondering what he was up to, but unable to turn him down. She'd tried, and failed miserably, and he'd shown her she didn't really know what she wanted anyway.

His hands on her back were a decadence, and she melted and purred as he massaged her muscles down to her butt. These bathing suits left them totally exposed, and even as she wore the one-piece today, it only covered her belly, leaving the rest of the suit held together with straps and strings.

Massaging the cheeks of her ass, he shifted the material to the side, exposing her fully. She arched her back in expectation of whatever pleasure he had in store, letting out a moan of agreement when she heard the rustle of fabric as shifted his own suit.

A suckling noise met her ears, and she realized he was wetting something to put inside her. Amelia relaxed her body, and allowed his thumb to breach her forbidden entrance. Up to the knuckle, he twisted and rubbed inside her, before pushing it all the way in with a groan. He lowered himself over her back, and whispered in her ear.

"I can't wait to put more in this tight little hole." His cock was between her cheeks from this position, and he thrust his hips to slide it back and forth. She couldn't stop the wriggle, pressing herself into him. From this position, he wasn't inside her, he simply rubbed against her folds and crevices, pumping back and forth. "I'm going to fuck your tits, too." His breaths turned ragged, but his words held a dark promise of a future with him. They were leaving this afternoon, so she knew he meant to do these things back home.

The only question for her was, would she be his dirty little whore at home?

As he took his pleasure from her body, the tightness of his thumb gave way to a slick pleasure. The taboo aspect of everything, the people on the beach not too far away, the fact he was in her ass, the public nudity, such as it was, all compounded to have her own breathing ragged and fast. She turned her head, and his hand was there, supporting him as he dove his hips across her skin, faster and faster.

It was pleasurable, but more because her body was making him lose his tightly reined in control. She opened her mouth, moved her head, and sucked his thumb into her mouth, grazing her teeth along the edge.

"Fuck," he moaned as he removed himself from her. Had she done something? "I need my cock in your mouth." She rolled over and leaned to where he was sitting, his cock poking out of his shorts.

She took him, using the same motions on him she had on his thumb. He grabbed her head and pushed it down and Amelia sucked for all she was worth, hollowing out her cheeks with the effort. He thrust his hips up so he was at the back of her throat, and his fingers stung her hair as he pulled with the effort to push her down.

She used her teeth as much as her tongue, scraping him on the way up, to give him that pain he seemed to need.

"Jesus, that mouth." The harsh, guttural utterance was more of a plea and it served to make her redouble her efforts. "Shit, fuck." Two hands on the back of her head. "Swallow. Work that throat."

He hadn't left her throat, and she gagged around him, sending moans and guttural curses to the sea. She couldn't breathe, and tears streamed down her cheeks as slobber spilled out of her mouth, wetting his shorts.

"Open wide." She did as she was told, and he pumped her face over his cock, until he roared his release into the back of her mouth without warning. It was actually sweet, with a salty tang, probably from the massive amounts of fruit they'd consumed all week. It was so like him, the walking contradiction of salty and sweet, although he didn't show the sweet in conventional ways.

When he let her up, he tugged her face up to his and kissed her hard. This was new. He kissed her plenty, but this was a kiss of gratitude, and as he swept his tongue inside her mouth, she felt like she'd made him the happiest man alive, if only for a brief moment.

Breaking the kiss, Charlie tugged her body into his lap. She enjoyed the physical closeness after their interludes. He would clutch her as if to make sure he was dreaming, his hands roaming and squeezing, massaging her body into a listless stupor. He was still breathing hard, but his dick was softening under her. Sweat stuck them together, in an intimate embrace, and she snuggled her head under his chin.

"I am wordless when it comes to you, Miss Flores. You make me do things that I've never done before, and it's fucking terrifying."

She giggled, because his words were making her uncomfortable. "You've never forced your cock down a woman's throat before?"

He chuckled at her response, but when he spoke, it was a whisper. "I've never fucking cuddled a woman before."

Shocked into silence, she simply let him. He'd cuddled with her after every single interlude since the first night after the bank. Even when they'd fooled around on the beach, they'd sat just like this, her in his lap, sharing a lounge chair.

Why did that make her feel absolutely giddy? Again, the giddiness faded into questions of what would happen when they got back to their respective homes.

She would soon find out.

CHAPTER SIXTEEN

Exhausted, Amelia managed to thank Luther before opening her door to get out of the car. Before she could leave, though, Charlie grabbed the back of her neck and tugged her into him.

"Thank you for this trip. It was … unexpected." Then he crashed his mouth into hers in a quick, harsh kiss that left her breathless.

A small smile graced her lips as she let herself into the house. It was almost dark, save for the one lamp in the living room. A woman sat in the easy chair, the nurse, but what was surprising was that she wore a long, heavy muslin skirt in a charcoal gray, with a long-sleeved button-up shirt. A mass of crochet sat in her lap.

Amelia cleared her throat to wake the woman.

Her eyes snapped open, and she jerked awake with a start.

Nancy was a retired ER nurse in her sixties, and Amelia had liked her from the start. She was kind, had an easy laugh, and a smoker's rasp, but she was efficient and knew what she was doing with Gram.

"I thought I said you could sleep in my room while I was gone?" Amelia had cleaned it and put all of her personal stuff away for the nurse to stay over while she was jet-setting with Charlie.

"You did, and I have, but I knew you would be home tonight and didn't want to get comfortable in your bed. I washed the sheets and everything this afternoon, so their fresh and waiting for you to pass out." The woman eyed her up and down. "You look really good. Sunshine agrees with you."

"Thanks. What are you wearing?"

Nancy laughed. "This old thing? An old costume when I was a WWI nurse for Halloween. Matilda seems to like it, so I've been playing along. She's sweet."

It was odd hearing Gram referred to by her given name, but Amelia appreciated the effort nonetheless.

"Is she doing okay?"

"She's fantastic! Her pickles are amazing. If it's alright, I can pass them around to some of my friends and bring back the jars for you. It would keep all of her hard work from going to waste."

A pang of guilt hit Amelia hard. "Yeah. I always wanted to do something with them. But the farmer's market can only sell so many, and the neighbors have all had their fill. I don't really have people I work with who would want that many of them. I've been at a loss as to what to do with them."

"Your gram really is amazing. I've seen several patients like her since I retired from the ER, and I've got to say, she's managed to build a world to live in that's positively lovely. Not a lot of dementia patients do that. You're lucky."

A small smile flitted across Amelia's face. Yeah, she was lucky. It had been a while since she'd thought of the reality of the dementia. Like Gram, it was preferable to just believe she lived in a completely separate world. Without Edwardian England, Gram didn't exist.

Nancy leaned forward and patted Amelia's knee as she rose from her chair. "We'll figure something out about the pickles. I'm going to go ahead and head home. Her chart's on the kitchen table if you want to see exactly what we've been doing. I'll be back Monday morning, bright and early. You have a nice weekend."

Amelia watched the woman bustle across the room and pick up her bag before waving her way out the door. She was enormously grateful for the lady. Wherever Charlie had found her, she was competent and friendly, and Amelia trusted her with Gram.

It was a nice break from worrying about her all day while she was at work.

Truth was, she'd said something that had Amelia thinking. The pickles were Gram's only remaining piece of reality. She'd told her long ago that the refrigerator pickles were her own mother's recipe, something she'd developed when they'd gotten their first-ever ice box. Even if it was a way to relive her past, it was a real past, not one that was made up to comfort her as her brain delved into whatever madness she lived in.

Amelia tiptoed down the hallway to her gram's room to find her sleeping soundly. A strange thankfulness she didn't have to make up something about where she'd been flitted through the disappointment at not getting this moment of her own normalcy with Gram tonight.

CHAPTER SEVENTEEN

Amelia had just shut the door to the car, and Luther had gotten back on the road again, when he started in on Charlie.

"Unexpected weekend, huh?" The laughter was clear in his comment.

"You're not supposed to be listening." Okay, he sounded like a petulant child. He didn't mind, though. Luther had been by his side since foster parents number six or seven. Granted, they'd spent some time apart, but they'd managed to keep in touch, and as soon as they'd both been sent to the group home until graduation, they'd escaped together.

"I like her." Luther said it quietly, but it meant more from Luther than anyone else. Charlie trusted his friend's opinion.

"Yeah. Me too." And he wasn't sure he liked it. "What place does she have with me, though? I can't really see myself settling down with kids and a dog, can you?"

Luther was quiet for a while. "No. Not the settling down part. You are who you are, and a woman's not going to change that. But she can soften it a little bit, yeah? It can't hurt things to have a conversation. See what she wants."

They had made it back into the city, and Charlie leaned back and thought about Amelia's life. It was so incredibly different from his. For her, he was a job she went to every day. The house he'd just dropped her off at was her home, her life. For him, his job was his life, his office his home. His apartment was the place he went every day.

What would it be like if Amelia was living with him?

"Hey." Luther got his attention in the rearview mirror. "You've done a lot in your life. You've risen from something dirty and impossible. I've seen you come back from some shitty odds, and actually do something with your life. You and Adam have done something incredible. You have been beaten, abused, all those clichés, but you're not where you came from. You have more money than you know what to do with. Who's saying you can't buy a fancy beach house and let her decorate it for you? Let her be your fucking partner and help you."

For the first time in his life, he imagined a woman in his kitchen. Stainless steel and black marble, it was cold and rarely used. Would her gram make herself at home, making those damned pickles? Would his cabinets be covered with Mason jars and cucumbers?

Amelia's glossy black hair would be a lovely contrast to the stark white of his bedroom. Her pale skin would be a complement to the monochromatic color scheme of his bed.

He imagined her draped over the arm of his leather couch, her skin heated and flushed from his spanking, sticking to the cold fabric of the furniture.

She'd probably put flowers everywhere. He found the thought not totally distasteful, as long as they were real, and not the plastic ones in her planter boxes.

"Yeah, I can see what she wants," he mused to himself, but Luther gave a grunt of approval.

**

Charlie showed up at Adam's warehouse at eight on the dot Saturday evening. Adam had this warehouse for the artwork he brought in from overseas, an occupation he'd inherited from his late wife. Adam's story was long and complex, and Charlie didn't want to dwell on it, even though up until now, it was way more interesting than his.

When he let himself in, Adam and Mack were there, with Luca standing off to the side. Adam had an office of sorts near the front of the building. The rest of the building with its crates and sheet-covered sculptures gave Charlie the creeps.

Dean knocked as soon as Charlie arrived, probably waiting for him to go in before he showed up in a room full of strangers.

They all sat around in the leather-bound chairs Adam had in his office, until Charlie got the ball rolling.

"Okay, we are all here for a mutual purpose, yeah? We can help each other accomplish it; we just need to be on the same page. That's what this meeting is for."

Charlie leaned back in his chair, crossing an ankle over a knee. Luca spun a high-backed chair backwards and straddled it. Mack leaned his back on two legs. Dean just sat in his stiffly. Charlie, the only one with a desk, leaned on it, resting his chin on one hand.

"We're ruining Forrester," Adam spoke with finality. Charlie knew this was on his mind at all hours of the day, and the dude probably had a plan in place. He was only modifying it to let these other guys in, hoping for a more dramatic resolution.

"Yes," Dean agreed on a hiss.

"Okay, so what do we want to do to him?" Charlie needed specifics so he would know how to steer the guys, since he was the facilitator.

"Utterly and publicly humiliated. Everyone in the city needs to know what he is," Mack spoke fiercely, and Charlie wondered idly how deep his hate was.

"He needs to be left with nothing. And no one." Dean spoke with a quiet intensity that was chilling.

Luca spoke up. "No money. No power. No self-respect."

Adam had a vague smile on his face, and it had grown bigger with each man's words. "In the end he'll have nothing. He will have time to reflect on the nothing he has left. And *then* we kill him."

None of the men flinched at the words, which told Charlie they were all on the same page.

Excellent.

"Okay. What is the skill set we're dealing with?"

"He's an investor at the local bank. On the board and all. It just went public and he has a shit ton of shares. I can take the bank down and drop the shares into an abyss of nothing." Mack spoke while smiling.

"How?" Adam asked idly.

"I've been working on a program that can siphon money out of bank accounts and put them into mine. It's subtle and gradual and nobody will know the difference."

"Okay, then what?" Charlie prodded.

Luca spoke up. "I've worked with him before. I know how his system works. I can hijack his shipments of drugs, women, and contraband. Resell them. Flush them. Whatever. He will lose his contacts that way if he's no longer a trustworthy distributor."

Charlie flinched at what was about to come.

"What the hell will you do with the women you steal from him?" Adam's voice was deathly quiet. It was his calm before his storm and Charlie knew he had to deflect this before he exploded.

"I can give them to Lola and help her get them back home." Charlie spoke up, giving Adam a name he trusted and helping him calm the fuck down. This was on the right track and didn't need a derailment. "Okay. Dean, what are your skills?"

"I don't really have many skills that don't involve brute force." Dean admitted, cracking his knuckles as he spoke. "I'm a vet who can't really talk to people, but I'm strong as an ox." He shrugged as he spoke.

"Okay, here's an idea. So far, we'll be hitting him where it hurts, his bottom line. If we cut him down at the knees, by hijacking his shipments, we can resell the stuff and take out his profit. If Mack's plan to drop the bank's shares works, he's losing money there. But what about this? His real estate development business is his daddy's bread and butter. He inherited that business when his dad died, and that is the legit face of his business." Luca stiffened as Charlie spoke. "He just made the business a publicly traded corporation last year. The shares still aren't that expensive yet. What if we bought out fifty one percent?"

They were all silent as they thought about that.

"Doesn't his daughter own ten percent?" Mack spoke up, and Charlie stiffened again. This was going to get hard with Adam on board.

Surprisingly though, Adam only smiled. "Leave that part to me. She won't be an issue."

"I don't have enough money to buy fifty-one percent," Dean said, obviously frustrated.

"Few of us do," Charlie replied. "But Mack can siphon off enough, and we can all put in money in various ways."

"I can start up some poker tournies in my back room," Luca said thoughtfully. "I'll have to make it a high buy in, but I think I can do it, if someone has any contacts with the cops."

"I do, even though Forrester's brother is the chief of police. There are enough that hate the two of them that it shouldn't be a problem paying a few to look the other direction."

"I can rob a few of his banks," Dean mused aloud. "Would that be enough for my part of things?"

"Not sure about financially, but you can help out with security at some functions and help with logistics of things."

"What about cleaning the money?" Mack asked. "You said we could do that."

"I've got some accounts overseas. Here's what we do. We put the money in those accounts, use the money to buy repossessed buildings at auction. Go to the bank and have them refinance the buildings so we can "fix them up," and voila! That money is clean. It's simple. Me and Adam have done it all before. Also, Luca can use his restaurant for some of the money. There are thousands of ways to clean it."

"We all need contingency plans."

Charlie clapped his hands together. "Okay, next time we meet, we will all have a plan for our part of things. From there, we will get an order of operations together, and I have a team building exercise in mind that will ensure we work well together."

"What the fuck?" Dean said just as Mack was dropping his chair onto all four legs.

"Team building?" Mack spat out.

"There is a lot of money involved in this, and most of us just met last week or tonight, so we need something to hold over each other to build trust. Non-negotiable." Adam just grinned at Charlie as he spoke.

"You are a wily son of a bitch," his friend said over his hand.

"You trust and believe in me for it, too. Now I just need these others behind us."

Luca sighed. "Just tell me where to meet next. I'm game for whatever it takes to take down the douchebag."

"A month from now. Everyone bring a business plan in writing for your part of this, along with a prepared financial statement of how much you intend to earn for your part." Charlie stood as he spoke and started walking out of the room.

He really needed to figure out what he was going to do with Amelia on Monday.

Charlie was going to need to clear his plate a little bit before all this started, because this would be a big job. Big, but worth it.

Amelia was throwing a cog in things though. He found he wanted to let her in, wanted her to know exactly what it was he did, so she could decide for herself if she was in or out with him.

Would it matter though? If she said she was out and couldn't do it with him, he wasn't sure he could just let her walk away. For one thing, she probably suspected too much about what he did for a living.

For another thing, he was pretty sure he couldn't let her go. He'd just gotten a taste of her, and there was so much more he wanted from her.

So much more.

**

The rest of the weekend flew by like normal. Amelia hit a low spot Saturday morning when she was washing her clothing from the trip. It was like a hangover after the best drunk of her life. The perfect vacation, playing all day, sexual tension, releases all night long, only to come home to her reality, and totally unsure of what Monday would bring. It was the uncertainty that was the worst, though.

She really had no idea what to expect when she went to work. She was pretty sure there wouldn't be an enormous bouquet of flowers on her desk, acknowledging the best week of her life.

No. That was not the sort of man Charlie was. Saturday afternoon, she had a moment of weakness and went shopping in the city for a surprise for him. Then she spent all day Sunday talking herself into actually using it.

CHAPTER EIGHTEEN

When Amelia got to the office Monday morning, she'd gotten her head on straight, prepared for whatever Charlie expected from her today. She knew what she hoped for, but she was unsure of things. The gift she'd bought Charlie left her with a delicious reminder of her hopes concerning him. And with every moment he didn't look at her, a definite disappointment.

Gingerly settling in her chair, she shoved her bag underneath the desk and checked his schedule for the day. It was becoming a habit she'd forced upon herself. Not because it was necessary, but because it was professional to not gape at visitors like a fish when they came in and announced an appointment.

He rarely had appointments come into the office, but today's calendar showed he was booked solid all morning. She looked up in surprise at him, staring through the window to his office. He was seated at his desk, his jacket off, but shirtsleeves rolled down and his cufflinks in place. His hair was as neat as it had been every morning he'd come in, like it was freshly combed.

He was not the island man she'd spent last week with. Not right now. Right now, he was the powerful businessman who got things done. And she wondered how long it would take him to notice her, her gift, or if she would just give up and go get rid of it before he noticed anything.

She squelched the feelings of desire she had flowing through her body at the memories of the week. He'd showed her things she didn't know she was capable of. And his actions had promised more dark delights to come.

Unfortunately, now, he looked busy, so she got up and made him a cup of coffee. She was desperate for him to look at her, be reminded of the things they'd done, feel some sort of warmth toward her again. Amelia was mightily disappointed he didn't seem to be thinking about it at all.

Running the coffee machine was a mindless task she could do, lost in her thoughts. Grinding, brewing, foaming, all of it a routine that settled her nerves. As she poured the foam into the cup, she created a forest scene for him, hoping to bring a smile to his eyes.

Then she felt ridiculous.

She was hoping for a smile from him. Attention. She was doing all of this for his attention. Especially the gift that she could feel with every movement she made.

Amelia rolled her eyes at herself. She would deliver his coffee, then go take the damn thing out.

No. It wasn't his fault she didn't know he had appointments scheduled all morning long. It was her fault for her expectations. He'd never told her they would continue their sexy times in the office.

With a sigh, she turned and walked to his office, balancing the cup and saucer without spilling or marring the intricate design.

The inside of his space smelled so strongly of Charlie, she practically gulped lungfuls of it as she walked around to the side of his desk to set the coffee cup down. He was on the phone when she entered, and he didn't stop talking, but his eyes followed her as he spoke.

When she turned to leave, he grabbed at her skirt, halting her with a hand on her hip. He tugged her backward a step, then ran his hand up the inside of her thigh.

"I can meet with you tomorrow morning, and we'll discuss this in more detail." His voice was normal, take charge, ask no questions, but his hand was seeking, on a quest for something.

Goosebumps erupted on her arms, as his rough fingers toyed with her garter belt before going to her ass. Her heart thumped in her chest while she tried to predict what he would do. He murmured mm-hmms in agreement to whatever someone said on the other end of the line, while his hand palmed her ass, his thumb slowly delved into the crack.

A sharp sensation of not-quite-pain-not-quite-pleasure rolled through her body with a shudder as his thumb bumped into the plug she wore.

"Shit, I've got to go. Call you back." Charlie slammed the phone into the cradle and used both hands on her hip, one under her skirt, one on top, to drag her closer to him. But he didn't look at her. She expected him to drag her skirt over her hips and stare at it, pull it out and do what she wore it for, or something. But he didn't. His hands gripped her tightly.

"What did you do, Amelia?" The question was quiet, but she heard the need. She leaned her hands on the desk and looked back at him, wanting to see his face.

It was focused on her ass, the gray material of her skirt, should have been see-through for all the exposure she felt right now.

"I—I bought a butt plug for you. You seem to be fascinated with my bottom, and I didn't want this last week to be a waste, soo—" She was saying too much. She was about to admit things she *knew* he didn't want to hear. "We started some things, and you promised to show me more. I was just helping it along."

She watched him swallow, his eyes in a daze. Slowly, he dragged his hand under her skirt down her leg, as if forcing it farther and farther away from her ass and the plug she wore.

"Do you want me to take it out?" She straightened, suddenly embarrassed. "I can go—"

He stood and spun her around. "Don't you fucking dare," he demanded. His mouth came down on hers hard and his tongue swooped inside her mouth quickly. She moaned into it, but it was over almost as soon as it started.

"I want you to go to the bathroom and take your hair down. Take off this skirt, turn around and take a picture. I want to see it, but if I look at it right now, I'm going to fuck you into next week, and I can't do that with the appointment I have coming in four minutes. But I will look at a picture of it for the rest of the morning. Then we're going to have lunch in here, my office, all over my desk."

The gritty hoarseness of his voice sent her reeling. It hadn't been a mistake. She gave him a smile, but he didn't smile in return. Instead, he reached for her breast and pinched the nipple. Hard. Amelia let out a harsh hiss of air, feeling the wetness pool across the inside of her thighs.

She was such a slut, wearing this, no underwear, for him. But his utter discomfiture at her doing it made everything worth it.

**

Charlie rubbed his face in disbelief. He'd been in here, trying to figure out how to open a dialogue with her, and she'd worked a goddamned butt plug into his office. How was he supposed to get anything done now?

He couldn't stop imagining her in the adult store, choosing one, taking it home and looking at it, wondering about it. He wished he could have put it in, but decided he liked this element of her surprising him.

It said so damn much, didn't it?

Right on time, Mack showed up and walked across Amelia's empty space to his office. Charlie forced himself to rise and shake the man's hand. He had business to tend to, and he needed his head on straight.

"I need someone to wire this office. I also have a list of things I need periodically throughout the course of my work. Do you know someone I can trust to do it?" He was talking fast, the knowledge of Amelia's actions making him antsy. It was a little uncomfortable, not something he was used to. But he couldn't help it. What she had done … shit.

"I can. I was a security systems installer in a past life. Since I quit doing that, I design my own systems and can do just about anything. Especially if you need remote wireless access."

They discussed particulars, and Charlie was barely coherent during the conversation, when his phone buzzed.

Like a schoolboy opening Christmas presents, Charlie grabbed his phone out of his pocket.

"One moment," he said to Mack, then looked at his screen. It was buzzing with multiple images. She was having a damn photo shoot in the bathroom.

He spun his chair around, putting his back to Mack and opened his screen. The first image was of her front side, wearing sexy-ass lingerie with the garters. Her face wasn't in the picture, and that was a disappointment. Quickly, he scrolled to the next one.

It was of her ass alone. A string around her waist and threaded between her cheeks, pushed to the side by a shiny, aquamarine colored jewel. He wondered if she chose it because it was the same color as the waters of Cayman.

The next picture was of her entire backside, taken in the mirror. She stood, legs spread apart, stockings and garters visible, and the aquamarine peeking from between her ass cheeks. She'd taken off her bra for this shot. Again, he couldn't see her face.

There were more pictures, images of her in the bathroom, nearly naked, her ass adorned with a jewel the color of the sea. For him. All for him.

He didn't deserve this woman.

But he wanted more.

"Everything okay?" Mack's voice from behind him brought him back to reality.

"Yeah. Everything's great." He spun around and found a place to settle his phone so he could see it and no one else. He needed to look at her to get through the morning.

He shuffled through some papers, occasionally glancing at his phone, as he found the list he needed Mack to fulfill.

"Here is the list. If you can get me this stuff, or do some of it for me, I'll skim some off the total cost of our prior deal with the other guys."

Mack's eyes lit up at the list, or the idea of Charlie cutting him a break in pricing. Either way, the guy looked amenable to doing this stuff Charlie had been needing.

"Also, I'd like you to go over the security system in the building, make sure it's up to standards."

"Sure thing."

"Great. I hate to cut this short, but I have meetings all morning and plans this afternoon." He glanced at his phone again, stifling the groan lodged in his throat.

Behind Mack, Charlie saw Amelia come through the door of the main office. She looked at him with heavy-lidded eyes before she took her seat at her desk wordlessly. He suddenly saw how she sat so carefully, scooting herself under the desk. He wondered how turned on she was right now.

"See you later, man. You want to come play poker with the guys Friday night? It's our first game, and we're going to make some plans you may want to be aware of."

"Yeah, sure." Charlie was still watching her, barely paying attention. "Text me a time and an address. I'll be there."

Mack's head spun around, seeing Amelia, and he chuckled to himself.

"I'll let myself out."

"You do that." His erection strained at the front of his pants and would give him away completely if he rose.

**

Amelia was more turned on than she could ever remember being. Her thighs were cramping from clamping them together so hard, and she was sure she was leaving a puddle in the chair beneath her.

The look on Charlie's face when he'd discovered her plug, and the heated glances he'd given his phone screen told her he was pretty close to being right there with her. Neither of them had stood from their respective desks since she'd come back inside the office, but she did wonder why he wasn't looking at her.

Client after client came in.

Her computer dinged a message from Charlie.

> Did you masturbate in the bathroom?

She smiled to herself as she typed two simple letters.

> How about this weekend?

She wasn't going to tell him how much she thought about it, but how weird it had seemed with Gram right next to her room. So she typed the word no again, and left it at that. He looked up at her then, and it took her breath away. He looked so damn turned on he looked angry, and a shudder of aroused anticipation went through her, so she added to her last message.

> Pretty sure it wouldn't take much at this point. This plug feels way better than I thought it would.

A look of determination passed over his face, and he said something to the man in the office with him. They both laughed, but Charlie looked strained. Then he typed again.

> Do it. Now. Under the desk. I want to see your face when you come.

Really? She mouthed the word, and he gave her a barely perceptible nod. Amelia took a deep breath, feeling her nipples press against the lace of her bra. Swiveling her chair, she inched her skirt up her thighs until she could reach herself.

Charlie's eyes darkened on her, and she realized he could stare at her and give a semblance of looking at his client, who sat in a chair directly between them. The back of his head and shoulder framed her image of Charlie's face as he watched her.

She reached up and pinched a nipple, hissing softly at the pain he'd taught her to love so much, then her other hand went to work, rubbing her clit in circles. She leaned back in her chair, putting pressure on the plug in her rear. She was so close. She hadn't been exaggerating when she'd told him that. It really didn't take much at all. She pinched her nipple again, releasing a soft gasp, then tugged on it gently while still rolling her clit under her fingertips.

Charlie's face faded into a blinding light that left her curled in on herself, one hand slapping on the desktop, while the other remained under her desk, hidden from his view, bringing herself down. But it wasn't fast enough. The orgasm hit her hard, then rolled around, leaving a dull ache in her core. When she was finally finished, she was gasping for air, and still horny.

She could do it again, right now. Well, she wanted to, but as she gave herself an experimental circle on her nub, the sensation ricocheted through her body, and she realized she was too damn sensitive.

Charlie stood, his open laptop blocking his crotch, as he leaned forward to shake his client's hand. She tried to straighten herself as best she could before the other man turned and saw her, but she was afraid the inner office smelled like her sex, anyway. She knew she probably had some sort of flush to her face that would give it all away, but he didn't seem to notice. He looked bothered and distracted, and she realized he had a problem he'd brought to Charlie to fix. Whether or not she had just gotten off under her desk was so far off his radar, she could probably be laid out naked right now and he wouldn't notice.

Her computer pinged again.

Lock the office door and get that beautiful ass in here.

She hurried to comply, her ass no longer stinging and burning. She'd stretched to accommodate the intrusion and now she felt only a fullness, a pleasurable pressure in her deepest, darkest places. She felt like she was moving with a slow sensuality that rocked it around inside her. She couldn't help the occasional roll of her hips, feeling it reach different places inside her.

When she got to Charlie's office, he had shut the laptop, and the bulge in his pants was remarkable.

He strode around the desk, taking her into his arms for an urgent kiss. He pressed against her lips and forced his tongue inside her mouth. She opened eagerly, mewling in pleasure, pressing herself against him wantonly.

"You're so full of surprises. I don't know what to do with you."

She was desperate for his touch. "Anything. Please." *I need you.* "Everything."

His arms clutched at her body, almost violently, but she loved it. His grip was hard on her breasts as he plumped them up and dropped his face to her cleavage. He ripped her shirt open, and she didn't care about the ripping noises and clatter of buttons as they hit the desktop and carpeted floor.

"I'm taking you now because I need it. But afterward, I'm taking that ass slowly. I've wanted it too long." His voice was rough, hard, and sent chills through her body. Desire coursed through her veins, and he could do anything to her and she would love it. She knew this about Charlie Delmonico.

He spun her around pushed her down on the desk, yanking her skirt up to her waist and tugging her thong aside. A low moan escaped from his lips as he played with his new toy. He twisted it, tugging it and pressing it back in place before thrusting his fingers inside the swollen lips of her core. He was relentless, and she was desperate. It was a combustible combination.

"Christ," he muttered as the jangle of his belt filled the room. She gripped the edges of the desk, her arms spread eagle and pressing her breasts against the top. She felt the cold of the wood through the lace, puckering her nipples. The head of his cock pressed against her entrance and slammed home, jiggling the plug with the motion. It sent sensations rocketing through her. She was incredibly full and could feel every ridge and curve and bump on his cock. He gave a muttered curse and started pumping in and out of her. Each thrust in was an invasion she welcomed, pressure everywhere, moving the plug from within. Each withdrawal was heartbreaking, leaving her bereft and needing more. One hand was at her hips, controlling his movements, as if he needed her help to do this. But the other hand toyed with the plug, continuing to press on it and tug. She was mindless with pleasure, about to die from the exquisite beauty of it all.

"Oh God," she said as another orgasm rippled through her. Her legs were shaking, and every muscle she had clenched tightly as he thrust inside her twice more, then stilled, coating her insides with his seed.

He was breathing so raggedly, she though he might keel over, but after a few moments, he recovered and pulled his still slightly erect member out of her.

"Now maybe I can take my time with this gift you've given me," he murmured as his finger traced a pattern on her ass, circling the plug, the circles growing smaller and smaller until he reached for it again and gave it a tug. The previous tugs had been experimental, this one purposeful. It came out, stretching her tight ring of muscles encircling it with a small popping noise.

Charlie kept her cheeks spread and she turned to find him looking at her darkest place in awe. It was almost like he couldn't believe what he was seeing, and she almost laughed. Surely women had let him do this before. He massaged her ass reverently.

"Did you bring lube?" She nodded.

"In my bag?"

He took a deep breath, then chuckled. "I'll risk it. Stay here and take off the rest of these clothes before I rip them to shreds. I'll find it and be right back." He yanked his pants back up and zipped them but didn't button them, then went to the office in search of her bag.

Naked aside from her stockings, garters, and shoes, since he seemed to like those, she leaned on the desk and watched him dig through her bag, his eyebrows furrowed in confusion as he searched for what he wanted. Emerging from her bag with the bottle of lube triumphantly, he practically jogged back to his office.

She waited for what was next.

CHAPTER NINETEEN

Charlie forced himself to halt inside the door to his office and just look at her. It was an offering, one he wasn't going to take lightly. He reminded himself she was new to all this. His world of pain and kinky eroticism was his alone, and the only women he'd been able to enjoy it with, were women he'd paid generously for the privilege. Before last week, she'd been an innocent. He'd played with her puckered little hole, but never satisfied himself with it.

Now, he would.

She had done everything he'd ever asked of her, right down to masturbating at her desk, so he could watch her come over the shoulder of Mr. O'Brian who was being blackmailed.

At first, she'd just been some little hot piece he hired so he could fantasize about ruining her. He had no idea she wanted to be ruined as badly as he wanted to do the deed.

She was a gift. He'd thought it once when he'd discovered the toy implanted in her asshole. Again, when she'd sent the pictures. Again, when he'd seen the rosy oh of her mouth as she came silently at her desk.

Now, as she leaned against his mahogany monstrosity, breathing heavily and looking a little fatigued after their previous foray, he thought it again.

A fucking gift.

And he wanted to look her in the eyes as he took her ass the first time. As he walked to her, he uncuffed the links at his wrists. Her eyes widened, and he realized he was stalking her. No matter. He couldn't stop himself. She was a gift, but she was his. And he was feeling a bit predatory. He'd make this good for her, but he was enjoying himself too much.

His cufflinks dropped on the desk behind her, and he unbuttoned his shirt, then unzipped his pants, letting them fall to the floor. She ran her hands up his chest and over his shoulders, taking off his shirt. He toed off his shoes.

Naked, he embraced her, feeling her warm, soft skin against his.

"Thank you," he murmured into her sweet-smelling hair.

She kissed at his neck, nipping it softly as she ran her hands down his back and grabbed his ass, pressing him toward her. She was cute if she thought she was in control of this situation.

A soft growl escaped his throat as he gently pushed her back on his desk, raising her legs from behind her knees and pushing them back. He slid her down so her delicious ass hung over the edge of his desk, and he curled her legs, pressing her knees practically to her ears.

"Hold them there," he demanded, his control on the thread of the edge of restraint. Reaching for the lube, he coated his dick, then his fingers, then poured it around her hole, gaping from her position and the plug. It was red, irritated, but it would look worse than this when he was finished.

Destruction. That was all on his mind as she whimpered while he coated everything, lubricating it. If he were a better man, he'd have insisted she graduate up to bigger toys before he stuck his dick in her there. The plug she'd bought was a small one, and he'd probably stretch her uncomfortably this time, but he couldn't go back in time and take back all the want he had for this moment.

There was no way he could stop this now.

He pressed the head of his cock against her forbidden entrance while rubbing circles on her clit. The noise she made was one of fear, and he leaned forward and took a nipple in his mouth, sucking and working it until she hissed in pleasure at him. He sank his fingers inside her pussy at the same time he pressed his head through the tight ring of her ass.

JesusfuckingGodChrist...

"So tight." That's what he thought he said, the garbled words coming out in a weird noise. Truth was, he was blinded by an ecstasy that bordered on pain, and it was delicious. A hand moved to her tit, molding it between his fingers, before tweaking a nipple to distract her from the pain. His other hand worked her clit to bring her pleasure.

It was automatic. All he could think about was getting deeper in there. He pushed forward more, an inch, as her eyes widened.

Hot. Smooth. So fucking tight.

Another inch.

"Do it," she gritted out between clenched teeth, and he looked at her face for the first time since he'd gotten her into position. The heat in her eyes was obvious, even with one lone tear leaking from her eye. Sweat beaded on her brow. She breathed with her mouth open, the breaths shallow and rough. So much innocence, breaking as he watched her.

He pressed in as far as he could go, almost to the hilt, then withdrew before pushing in again. Leaning over, he licked the tear from her cheek and nearly lost control.

Settling into a slow rhythm, he forced himself to not slam into her virgin asshole today. She closed her eyes and her head fell back. Moving her forearms under her knees, she reached for her own nipples.

"Fucking God, yeah. Do that." She stimulated her nipples and he went to work on her pussy, drawing his fingers through the accumulated wetness from the both of them there.

This wasn't going to take long for him, and he needed it to be good for her.

He pumped his fingers in and out of her, three of them, until he could feel himself through the thin wall separating the two holes. He muttered more curses as her sounds of pleasure got louder, turning into wails. He pressed his thumb against her clit, trying to rub, but unable to concentrate on everything at once. It felt too good.

Pleasure was building at the base of his spine, and he felt his balls draw up. He knew he was going to come quickly if he didn't do something soon.

He froze his hip movements and concentrated on her pleasure for a minute, finding the spot inside her that would make her fly apart. He watched her eyelids widen, her mouth fall open, and then felt the shudder of her pulsing climax.

And he thrust hard, three times, four times, his pelvis slapping into her ass. He roared his release as he felt the explosion inside him. It came in torrential waves of bliss as she tightened around him like a vise. He couldn't move, he couldn't see, blood roared through his ears.

Jesus Christ.

She shook on his desk as he withdrew from her, but he wanted to hold her, so he picked her up and settled in his chair, laying her on his lap. She curled into his body, and he stroked her back, relishing the utter mess he'd made of her body.

It was a glorious marking, lube and his seed leaking out of her holes. Sweat and tear tracks covered the skin of her face, sweat also dripping down her back and shoulders.

She trembled in his arms, and he shushed her. He was about to do something he'd never, ever done before, and he didn't even think twice about it. At this point, it was necessary.

"Come home with me tonight."

She nodded her acceptance, and as soon as his voice was normal again, he called the nurse, asking if she could stay with Gram for the night, then he called Luther and told his driver he was ready to go home. Then he walked to his closet and found Amelia one of his shirts to wear home. It was obvious what they'd been up to in his office, even with her skirt under it, but the massive shirt was so clearly not hers, or anything she would ever wear.

Still, he liked it on her.

She was silent as they took the freight elevator down and got into his car.

CHAPTER TWENTY

Quiet on the drive, they were both lost in their own thoughts, but it didn't miss his observations she silently wept on the way. He reached for her, wanting to say something, but not in front of Luther. For the first time ever, he wished he had a privacy screen to block his friend out of the conversation he longed to have with Amelia.

She accepted his touch, though, and wove her fingers in his, squeezing almost painfully. So she didn't regret things, he didn't think. She needed his touch.

He scooted over and wrapped her in his other arm, and she buried her face in his chest. He felt the hot wash of her beautiful tears as she wept silently into his shirt, continuing to clutch her hand to her chest. It rested between her breasts and didn't even twitch.

Right now, things had transcended sex with him, and he didn't know what to do with that reality.

When they got home, he thanked Luther for driving them, and told him he'd call in the morning when he needed him. Then he got out and helped Amelia inside his building.

They rode the elevator up, again in silence. She still clutched his hand.

Unlocking his door, he led her inside and over to the couch immediately. He sat her on the plush sofa and asked words he never thought he'd speak to a woman.

"What do you need?"

Surprise flickered over her face as she looked at him. She hadn't expected the question either.

He wanted to talk about this. What had happened, and miraculously, he wanted to talk about where they would go now. He needed them together, and he didn't want to let her go. She was his, and he needed her to understand that.

"I don't know." She worried her lips with her teeth and he watched, fascinated. Her eyes watered again, and he mentally urged the tears to fall, so he could witness it. "I want you. I want sleep. I want food."

He stood, his hand still grasping hers as tightly as she held his.

He felt like he was in junior high, trying to impress his first girlfriend. But he didn't give a shit. He took her into his bathroom and sat her on the toilet while he drew a bath. He found some oils and put them in the water, making it as hot as he dared. Then he carefully stripped her bare and led her into the water. From outside the tub, he washed her body, starting at her feet and massaging and rubbing gel into her skin, relishing the feel as her muscles relaxed under his touch.

Things with Amelia were so different. Before her, he'd never rubbed anything into a woman's skin. Now, he wanted to rub everything into her skin. He loved massaging her while he listened to the satisfied sounds coming from her mouth.

He washed her hair, twice, enjoying the silky strands as they fell through his fingers. He rinsed it the final time, using the detachable shower nozzle.

She had stared at him the entire time. In the mirror that lined the walls around the tub, he watched her eyes follow him as he moved. It was almost like she needed to see him, to know he was real.

He held out his hand to help her out of the tub, drying her with a fluffy towel and leading her into his bedroom and over to the bed. He wanted to see the reality of her against his sheets.

She looked tiny in his massive bed, but it seemed to suit her. He kissed her forehead as he settled her in.

"I'll go get some food. Be right back."

**

Those were the last words Amelia heard before she closed her eyes. The day was overwhelming and after the bath, her fatigue had taken over her hunger. The bed was soft, the sheets cool, and the pillows heavenly.

The next time she opened her eyes, the room was dark and a heavy weight held her down. She threw the down comforter off and realized the weight wasn't the blankets. Charlie was draped over her, his arms snuggling her to his chest, his legs tangled in hers. She was naked, but he wore a pair of sleep pants. His soft snores in her ear were soothing noises that almost lulled her back into dreamland.

But then her stomach growled at her, and she carefully peeled his arm off her and disentangled her legs before getting out of bed and grabbing one of his t-shirts from a nearby hamper. She needed to find some food.

His apartment was massive. As she silently moved around it, the moonlight filtered in through windows to light her way. She saw a living room larger than her house, and beyond it, the kitchen, lit up by a light over the stove. She used it to maneuver her way around, finding a huge sandwich on a plate in the refrigerator wrapped in cling wrap. He must have made that for her when she'd fallen asleep.

A happy squeal escaped as she grabbed the plate and took it to the counter. She stood over the sink and ate. She didn't stop when she heard the thudding of feet as Charlie stormed through the apartment.

He'd woken.

Anticipation at seeing him again ratcheted her nerves, but she didn't have long to enjoy the tingle, as his legs were long enough to eat up the floors between them in a matter of seconds.

"I thought you'd left me." She turned at the sound of his voice, her mouth full. He looked desperately lost and it reached out and clamped down on her insides, almost painfully. As his eyes traveled down her body, though, it seeped out of his expression.

She looked down, realizing how she must look, mussed from sleep and wearing nothing but one of his t-shirts. It still smelled like him, and she decided he must work out in it, since it smelled vaguely of a clean sweat. She hadn't noticed before, since she'd been intent on navigating her surroundings and finding food.

"I tried not to wake you."

He walked closer and leaned on the cabinet next to her, watching her with a careful look on his face.

"My alarm went off."

"What time is it?"

He shook his head. "Motion sensor."

For a moment she'd forgotten who she was dealing with. Yesterday had been a sort of dream for her, one she'd walked through in a fog. But it was real. She'd done things with Charlie, her boss, she'd never dreamed of doing. Like an out-of-body experience, she remembered everything.

Even now, it made her blush with arousal.

His mouth quirked as he noticed, but thankfully, he didn't make a move to do anything about it.

"Let's talk about yesterday, shall we?" His arm muscles bulged as he used them to jump on the countertop and sit.

She stuffed the last piece of sandwich in her mouth and leaned on the counter next to him while she chewed.

"I don't know what came over me to do all that." She wasn't going to apologize, even if he expected it. She wasn't sorry. The only thing that would make her apologetic was if he turned her away because of it. But she didn't think he would.

He put a finger over her lips as she spoke though, indicating he wanted to go first. Okay, she'd let him.

She pressed her lips together and waited. He took a deep breath and let it out slowly.

"I know it has crossed your mind since you came under my employ that I was paying you for sex. And that is most definitely not the case. Like I told you before, that's not what I was paying you for." He took another deep breath and she knew whatever he was about to say was hard for him. "Yesterday … yesterday was … I don't have words for what yesterday was. Exquisite, thrilling, fucking bliss. All of it, more." He bit his lip and shook his head. "I have no idea what you want from me. I'm not a good guy, and I have never, ever had a relationship with a woman. But I want one with you." He looked at her, really looking into her eyes, and the intensity of the emotion in the dark depths was like nothing she'd ever seen before. "I want everything with you. Your happiness, your pain, your pleasure, your tears, your laughter, your memories. But I need you to accept me for who I am. I can't change. I'm a devil, and I lied before when I said I wouldn't hurt you. I can't help it. I'll hurt you without meaning to, because that's who I am. Sometimes the shadows take over and I do shit. That's why I'm in the business I'm in. So I can hurt people and get paid for it."

She had an idea what sort of business he was in. She'd gleaned enough from working with him.

"But you wouldn't hurt me the way you hurt the people you get paid to hurt. That's the difference. You're talking about a different kind of hurt from the physical hurt. That's what I thought you meant in Cayman." She remember the conversation, and how opposite it was to this one right now. A thrill of excitement ran through her and she couldn't stop the smile that spread across her face. She moved over to stand between his knees. "What you're talking about wanting with me is what people in committed relationships get with each other. The commitment to share everything. The good, the bad, and the ugly."

"But I find beauty in ugliness. That's what I mean. I may hurt you so I can see that beauty." He leaned his head on the cabinet behind him.

That was how he found his pleasure, and she was okay with that. Especially if yesterday was an indicator.

"I didn't know things could feel like that, Charlie," she said quietly. "Yesterday. I was going to do it, because I wanted to please you. I knew it would hurt, but I underestimated how much. But I also saw everything you've been trying to tell me about pain and pleasure. It was good because it hurt so much. The pain made the pleasure so much more."

"So, if you don't want a committed relationship with me, I'll pay you to continue the way we are. I need it, Amelia. I didn't realize how much." He gripped the t-shirt she wore, tugging her closer. A smile tugged at her lips at his misunderstanding. "I need this with you. I will have it."

His touch became needier, as if having her closer to him broke some sort of dam. His forehead touched hers as he leaned over her, gripping her ass in his hands. "This was a gift I'll never have a hope of getting that way again."

"I don't know how you got the idea I don't want a committed relationship with you. I lo—care about you, Charlie Delmonico." She almost slipped and said something she couldn't come back from and she was sure he wasn't ready for. She pressed a kiss against his mouth as he opened it to say something. "I'll do what you want. You want my tears? Lick them off my face. You say you're a devil, but I see the goodness in you, every time you touch me. I see you."

He growled as he took her mouth, leaping off the countertop and wrapping his hands around her waist. With one motion, he had her over his shoulder and he carried her to his bedroom.

CHAPTER TWENTY-ONE

A few hours later, sunlight tried to squeeze through the cracks of his curtains, creating all sorts of interesting shadows on Amelia's face while she slept. Charlie was torn between waking her for the office, and watching the shadows change on Amelia's face as the sun crept higher in the sky.

After he'd carried her back to his room, he'd taken his time with her. He couldn't say he was exploring her body, since he'd been learning about her for a week, but he certainly found new ways to pleasure her. A gentler way, something he'd never actually done before.

He'd been slow. Giving instead of taking. He could still hear her moans of pleasure as they reverberated through his room.

Charlie had been sweet, and he'd actually liked it almost as much as his usual way. He laughed to himself as he reached for a tendril of dark hair and pushed it off her face.

Yet, he still didn't know anything about her. Not about her fears, her passions, aside from his new coffee maker. He didn't know anything about what scared her.

And for some reason, now he wanted to know. At first, he'd wanted to see her fear so he could feed off of it in some weird way. But now, he wanted to banish it, so she never had to be afraid again.

"What scares you, Amelia?" he asked in a whisper, more to himself than to the sleeping figure beside him, but she answered him anyway. She must have heard him in some dream state.

"Jackson," a shaky voice coming out as a fearful moan answered him as she pulled the covers tighter around her neck. A protective gesture, it made his fist clench.

Every muscle inside him tensed. A man scared her? Suddenly, so much made sense. Her flinching when he was angry or made quick movements. Her morphing from aroused to terrified, when he'd first brought up his penchant for pain with his bed play.

So many little things. This Jackson guy had actually physically hurt her. Scared her.

"Jackson who?" He growled, no longer having the option to let her sleep. He needed an answer.

Amelia came awake with a start, her eyes darting around the room wildly until they settled on Charlie and relaxed into a half-awake state.

"Jackson who? I need a last name."

"I was dreaming. I'm sorry. He's nobody." She rolled over and snuggled up to him, her warm softness plastered against his side.

But for once, he wouldn't be distracted.

"What did he do to you?"

Her head turned against his shoulder and she realized he wasn't going to let it go. She sighed, closed her eyes, and said, "Fine. Ex fiancé. I got pregnant and he wanted me to abort it. When I wouldn't, he beat me until I miscarried." A tear leaked from her eye, and instead of licking it away, a red rage burned at him at the sight of her tears caused by another man.

Tears he caused were different than tears this douchebag did. Still, they were both Amelia's pain. And he was going to do something about it.

"Last. Name."

Her lip quivered as she sat up, holding the sheet to her chest. A knowledge sat heavy in her eyes as she looked at him with recrimination. She knew exactly why he wanted the man's name, and there was nothing she could do about it.

"If you don't give it to me, I'll find out another way." He tried to gentle his tone, but he couldn't help the anger that burned through. He was more than pissed. The red haze he'd initially felt was seeping into his vision, clouding the edges.

"Braxton." No more than a whisper, but he took it and held on to the feeling of retribution that settled into his gut. He had a name, and he knew exactly what to do with it. Only douchebags had two last names.

"Get dressed. I'll have Luther drop you at home." Without another word, he slid out of bed and stalked to the shower, a new purpose in his step.

**

Luther drove her home in blessed silence. What was Charlie going to do? Last night had been so beautiful, and she had no idea why she had messed everything up by saying Jackson's name out loud. She'd been dreaming something pleasant, probably about the beach and sunshine, and then Jackson had suddenly appeared, unbidden.

He was a horrible person, but for a brief moment in time, he'd been kind enough to her that she'd wanted to spend her life with him, start a family with him. The monster hadn't shown up until he felt trapped. That was human nature, wasn't it?

She was afraid Charlie would kill him, and then his blood would be on her hands.

She had to stop him.

When Luther pulled up in front of her house, she leaned forward.

"Wait for me, please? It won't take me long to shower and change. I need to go back and stop Ch—Mr. Delmonico."

Luther chuckled. "You can try, but he's in a mood. Not sure you'll be able to."

Luther probably knew Charlie better than she did. He'd certainly known him longer.

"I have to try."

"Fair enough. I'll wait."

CHAPTER TWENTY-TWO

Amelia was not prepared for what happened next. Nothing could have prepared her. Even with everything she knew about Charlie as a "fixer" or whatever, she never could have reconciled the Charlie who had been so tender, so demanding, so sensual, with the cold man who waited for them at the front of his office building.

He didn't speak as he got into the car with her, simply nodded at Luther.

"So you decided to join us?" He said it as he looked at her, then he faced forward again. "Should be educating for you." His jaw ticked as he clenched it.

She could ask all sorts of questions, probably should, so she would know what to expect, but a part of her already did. The sinking part that despaired and screamed at her to stop him. But she didn't know how, and as she thought about Jackson and what he'd done to her, she wasn't sure she wanted to.

Jackson had betrayed her. He'd been a golden boy, showering her with love. He'd convinced her to quit school, three years into college, and marry him. They made plans, and she moved in with him. The plans were so consuming, she suddenly found she had no time for her friends. She barely saw her own family. But his were with her constantly. His mother helped her plan, choosing flowers, cakes, the church, everything. She was paying for most of it, after all, as she was constantly reminding her.

When Amelia ended up pregnant, it clearly messed with Jackson's plans for himself. He couldn't be a prelaw student with a baby at home. Apparently, he never wanted kids, but hadn't deemed it necessary to tell her.

He'd been so angry. She'd been hospitalized for days, recovering from the beating. Thankfully, one of the nurses had called her grandma, and she'd picked Amelia up before Jackson could get there.

She hadn't seen him since.

Something had happened to Amelia in that hospital room. She'd changed from the naïve woman who dreamed of being Jackson's wife and doing whatever he wanted to a woman who'd lost her way, but was anxious to get back on track.

Unfortunately, when she'd quit school, she'd lost her financial aid. But that was the least of her worries. At least now she was free from Jackson. Right?

So she'd started over. Forgotten him and all the mistakes she'd made. And she was happy now.

And Charlie was bringing it all back to her.

Luther pulled up in front of the house that was supposed to have been hers and Jackson's. It was a house she'd honestly never thought she'd see again. Charlie practically bounced out of the car, forgetting her in his excitement. She'd never seen him like this before.

His mouth was set in a grim determination, but there was a light in his eyes. It was a bit scary, the spark of danger that peered back at her when she called his name. The glint of danger actually made him look younger, full of life.

It made her stop short. She watched him over the top of the car as he went to the trunk and opened it. When it slammed shut, she saw a wooden baseball bat in his hand. It was old, but looked worn, oiled with care.

She swallowed, imagining what he was going to do with it.

"Insist on seeing this?" He finally looked at her. She nodded, eyes not leaving the bat.

The bat twirled in Charlie's massive grip, light as a feather.

He rang the doorbell and stood there, bat placed between his feet, hands resting on top of it, as if it were a cane or something. Amelia couldn't take her eyes off it.

Jackson answered, groggy from sleep. If he'd followed his plan, he was taking classes still, so didn't have a regular 9-5 schedule.

As a college student, he'd probably stayed up all night partying.

"What?" He rubbed his eyes.

"Classy." Charlie looked over at Amelia, and she smiled warily. Jackson wore his boxers and an enormous tank top that showed off skinny arms.

"What the hell are you doing here?" Jackson was looking at her, as if the suited man with the baseball bat wasn't standing there. Charlie pushed him inside his house with a growl. "What the fuck, man?"

"I don't have many rules, but beating women is one of them. So I'm here to give you a choice."

"I don't know what she said about me. Bitch is a liar."

Charlie held the baseball bat carelessly in one hand, while he pulled a gun out from under his jacket. Amelia's eyes were riveted to the gleaming black piece of metal he waved in front of Jackson's face.

"Charlie, stop," she gritted out between clenched teeth.

"You can have a quick death. Easy, painless. Or you can take a beating you might survive, but it will hurt a hell of a lot more." Charlie had Jackson crowded against the wall of the foyer.

He was going to *kill* him?

"Wait, Charlie. Please." She reached for his arm to tug him back, but he sidestepped her effortlessly, going back to crowding Jackson.

Amelia stood next to the table she'd chosen from the Pottery Barn catalogue, imagining a new vase of fresh flowers on it every week. Now, it didn't have flowers on it. It was empty.

"Charlie, don't." Her voice held less fear than she felt. It was weird. She was wooden. She wanted to reach out and grab the gun, but she'd never held a gun before and the idea of having the cold metal in her hands made her not want to do that. The baseball bat she could grab, he held it loosely enough. But she didn't. And she didn't know why.

"Fuck you, man. You can have her. I don't want her anymore. It's been years since I did."

That hurt a little, the incident had only happened a year and a half ago. But he had a gun waving around his face; he was probably lying to save himself.

"Not what I asked. I gave you a choice. Pay attention." His choice was death or hospitalization. How fair was that?

As if he suddenly realized the seriousness of the situation, Jackson finally focused on the gun in his face. Charlie tucked it under his chin.

"Pain? Or death?"

"Please!" She was louder, no longer hissing between her teeth. She didn't want to get in the middle of this, but she didn't want it to happen either.

"Look, my parents have money, I can get you what you want."

"I have what I want. And she hurts because of you. Now fucking choose, or I'll do it for you." Charlie's voice was calm, low, but deadly. A shiver coursed through Amelia.

When Jackson didn't say anything, Amelia saw what was happening. She watched it all in a weird daze. Very calmly, Charlie put the gun back in the holster under his jacket. He shrugged it off and handed it backwards to Amelia, who took it automatically. One at a time, with the bat under one arm, he undid his cufflinks, handing them back to Amelia as well. Then he started rolling up his sleeves.

Amelia took a step sideways, getting herself out of the way, yet granting herself an excellent view of Charlie's face.

Grim with determination. Danger still glinted from his eyes, but the anticipation was gone, and so was the light. Amelia was cold. She hugged his jacket to her body while hugging herself, unable to stop what was happening, nor look away from it.

She loved Charlie, but how far would that take her? As he raised the bat over his shoulder and swung with a grunt, she heard Jackson's yell, the smack of wood on skin, the crunch of bones, and her own teeth chattering. It was an amalgamation of noises in the silent house.

As Charlie methodically beat Jackson with the baseball bat, his harsh breaths overriding the other man's diminishing voice, she felt nothing but the cold.

"Stop," she whispered, hearing the futility of the non-gesture. But she couldn't be louder. Suddenly, it was all too much. The noises in the room too loud. Too cold.

It seeped through her clothes, chilling her to the bone. The base savagery of Charlie was because of her, she'd made this monster, and she had no idea how. Was it the dream Jackson had only been in for a split second before she'd awoken? Whatever it was, she had caused this monster to emerge from Charlie.

His motions were smooth, as he brought the bat back, then forward, only jerking to a halt when it met with Jackson's body. He was curled up on his side, bleeding and whimpering, a shell of the man she'd once thought would be her happiness.

She realized she was flinching with each sickening thud of the bat against flesh. Charlie's shirt had come untucked, and his shirt bunched around the holster around his arm. She focused on that to keep from thinking about what she watched. The fine fabric, wrinkling around the leather and elastic of the holster. It all fit him well, if she hadn't been watching him beat Jackson to death, she might find it sexy.

But right now, she was fighting the nausea rising in her throat.

She had no idea if Jackson lived or died. Everything else was flashes of memory, Charlie finishing up his destruction, leading her to the car, the suppleness of the leather seats.

The city zooming by as she leaned her head against the window.

Luther's pitying eyes in the mirror as he glanced at her.

Charlie's cold demeanor.

She retched, bile thick in her throat, as her stomach turned upside down.

"Please pull over, Luther." He obliged and she opened her door and threw up on the street, chunks of whatever remained in her stomach after that late-night sandwich she'd eaten an eon ago. The bile of what she'd seen.

Her eyes focused on her surroundings, figuring out where she was. She reached back into the car and grabbed her bag.

"I'll call a cab home." She risked a glance at Charlie as she spoke. He watched her, his eyes looking tortured.

"I'll walk to the office; Luther can take you home." His voice was hoarse, and she couldn't be sure if it was from yelling at Jackson while he beat him to a pulp, or if it was remorse. She didn't remember him yelling at Jackson, though.

And she doubted it was remorse. He'd had opportunities to stop, but hadn't.

Amelia shook her head, her hand in a white-knuckled grip with her shoulder bag. "I need to walk for a while. I have money for a cab."

Charlie nodded.

Amelia slammed the door shut.

She stepped over her vomit and walked down the street. There was a park here somewhere. She was in a foggy daze as she found it and sat on a bench. She didn't notice Luther pulling the sleek town car up to the curb to wait for her.

"Are you alright?" A jogger pulled her out of her thoughts.

"Of course," she replied, not fully comprehending where she was.

"You have some blood …" He pointed at her chest, and she looked down. The white blouse she'd worn today to the office had blood spatters on it.

"Not mine."

A short beeping honk drew her attention to the car idling at the curb. Luther was waiting for her.

"Amelia," he called to her, loud enough to be heard, but soft enough to not scare her. She appreciated it. "He walked. Get in."

She supposed that was just as well. A cab ride home would cost close to a hundred dollars.

Ensconced in the back seat, she let out a heavy sigh.

"I'm just going to say one thing, and then I'll be quiet the rest of the drive," Luther began, his voice soothing, as if she were a wild animal. She supposed he was used to talking to Charlie this way. "I've known him a long time, and he's never taken to a woman like he has you. What he did today wasn't for himself. It was for you."

"He did that for me?"

"I can tell it was misguided, but his dark heart was where he thought it should be."

Luther, true to his word, was quiet, until they were almost home. As he pulled into her neighborhood, he spoke again. "We both like you, Miss Amelia. Of course, he loves you. And I love you by proxy. I haven't seen him smile the way he has these last couple of weeks. You will be good for him, if you try."

She was surprised she wasn't crying, but she was sniffling, trying to keep back tears. She wasn't sure she wanted to try at this point.

"I don't think I can, Luther." When he put the car in park, she paused before opening the door. "Thank you for everything."

"I'll see you." He gave her a soft smile, and she didn't have the heart to tell him she didn't think he would. That he was the only man who ever had.

CHAPTER TWENTY-THREE

Charlie walked to his apartment and changed before heading to the office. While Luther drove him nearly everywhere, he actually lived only a few blocks from where he worked, so it wasn't a long hike.

Yet it gave him time to think.

He didn't regret beating the man who'd hurt Amelia, but he regretted the consequences of the action. However, it was who he was. She needed to see it now, before she got in too deep. She thought she loved him, she'd told him so, but now there was no way she could.

He, on the other hand…

If she'd been pregnant with Charlie's child, there was no way he would be so stupid as to ever do anything to make her leave him. He would turn into a ridiculous sap who doted on her every need, want, and desire. He would be putty in her hands.

That guy didn't deserve a second glance from her, much less to be her husband.

Charlie tried to lose himself in work, confirming plans, making new ones. Now that the mayoral opposition was taken care of, Savage's ratings were high, and he was sure to win his candidacy. The payment had come through in his account, and now he only had to start in on the high school football player's reputation before colleges started dropping him. The kid's parents were rich, but he'd been busted breaking into someone's house.

Charlie was tempted to let the kid ride it out, claim the job impossible, let him live with his consequences. He couldn't imagine a good scenario where he learned from his mistakes and turned out to be a good human after Charlie repaired things with the public perception.

But it was a paycheck, and this was what Charlie did. So he made a few phone calls, spoke with the kid and told him where to be when, and got the ball rolling.

One of the women on his payroll, Lola, would be in the wrong place at the wrong time, and the kid would be there to save her. A web-extra reporter would also be there with his camera, coincidentally doing a piece on neighborhood crime and would capture the entire thing on camera.

The kid would be touted as a local hero, a romance would blossom between him and Lola, and Charlie would set up some charity work for the kid to start doing with children who get in trouble with the law. He would amend his ways and turn over a new leaf. Yada yada.

Reputation restored. Hopefully the colleges would continue fighting over who got to have him start as their quarterback in the fall.

His work would be done. But then again, who really gave a shit if one more petty criminal got away with stealing the family's silver?

He didn't. But the kid's parents were willing to pay a small mint for it, so who was he to question it?

Even through his work, his thoughts kept straying to the events of this morning. He couldn't have changed his actions if he tried, but he knew without a doubt that they had lost him the person who was quickly becoming more important to him than Luther, his best friend since childhood.

No, he couldn't have changed the events from today any more than he could turn his skin green. It wasn't just the beating, although that probably would have caused it easily enough. But the reasoning behind it, a pregnancy, tipped him over the edge of reason. What would he give for the chance to see Amelia's belly swell with his own child inside of her?

Offspring weren't something he'd ever imagined for himself. But with her? Absofuckinglutely.

She was the only woman he possibly could imagine it with.

And for that asshole to take it for granted like that was unthinkable. He was a murderer, in every sense of the word.

He couldn't imagine Amelia's pain when it had happened. It was the stuff of nightmares, and he wished he could have been there for her, to witness it, to absorb it and take it away.

No wonder she fucking flinched.

It was a subconscious protection thing, her curling of her body inward, an attempt to protect herself from unseen dangers.

A heavy weight sat on top of his chest, making it difficult to breathe. He wasn't sure exactly what it was, but he had an idea. Different from his usual adrenaline crash after a well-deserved beating, it filled his limbs with lead. It was the crushing weight of anticipated despair. She would leave him. She had left him, hadn't she?

Because she was a good woman and couldn't be with someone like him. She needed a good man, a doctor, or humanitarian, or someone of that ilk. He was certainly not that man.

He needed to let her go to find that man.

It hurt, and he hated it. His own pain was something he'd said goodbye to a long time ago. It had been a conscious decision to not feel it ever again, to not feel small from the ridiculous emotion of emotional pain.

But he welcomed it now.

He surveyed his desk, his office with its glass walls. His domain. He'd built this.

Charlie suddenly didn't want to be here.

He wanted to go to his apartment, smell his sheets, see her imprint on the pillow from this morning, before everything fell apart.

Then he would wash the sheets to get rid of that memory, and he would put her out of his mind. There was no need to dwell on her. He had things to do and accomplish, and he knew now, he couldn't do it with her.

**

Amelia didn't have the heart to even call and quit. It was just too much, the idea of hearing Charlie's voice again, knowing the disappointment she would feel because she hadn't been able to handle him.

So she took the chickenshit way out. She didn't call him to say she wasn't coming back. She didn't give him a piece of her mind for doing what he'd done to Jackson. She did call 9-1-1 to tell them there was a man in distress at his address, but nothing more.

She ran and hid in her home to lick the wounds of being yet again, too little, too much, just not right for someone.

Of course, the nurse was there, sitting with her crocheting in the easy chair.

"You can go. I'm not sure about tomorrow, but I'll call you." Her voice pleaded with the friendly lady to not argue with her. She didn't want to explain that the man who'd hired them both was a vile man.

Even if those words didn't quite describe him. She wasn't going there, not even in her head.

She opened her mouth to respond, but snapped it shut, smiling vaguely instead.

"I understand." She rose and gathered her things to leave. "But please, keep me updated. I don't mind coming in for a reduced price, if you need me to."

Amelia was grateful for the gesture, but she didn't think it would help. She was currently unemployed and didn't think she'd find a job with no degree that would afford the kind woman's efficient care.

She had no job. Gram needed tending. And she was suddenly overwhelmed and frustrated.

When the woman left, Amelia went into Gram's room to remind herself of her goals.

She'd completely lost sight of them with Charlie.

Gram was resting for the afternoon. She napped in the afternoon most days, after her grand pickle-making endeavors. Today was no different, except she sat up with a book in her hand.

"You're home early." Gram looked at her with one raised eyebrow and Amelia was surprised the woman was aware she wasn't supposed to be here, much less what time of day it was.

"Well, I broke my engagements to spend a little time with you over the next few days."

"Quit your job, you mean? Downtown businesses don't usually let employees take time off to visit home."

Amelia stifled the gasp that wanted to escape. Gram didn't observe her need to work a real job when she was stuck in her regency romance world.

"Yes. I quit."

"What happened with Mr. Delmonico? You seemed rather taken with him, as I recall. Although my memory isn't what it used to be. I could be remembering wrong."

Amelia's mind raced. Number one, Charlie had only been here once, and that was before they'd done anything together. Number two, Gram didn't remember *anything* right, so the idea she was getting this at all was almost laughable.

"We didn't … mesh." She settled for the understatement, seeing the lie for what it was. Physically, they'd meshed so freaking good. Her skin heated at the thought.

"I see, well, you'll need another job, then. Yes? And don't worry about the meshing aspect of things." She said the word as if it tasted bad.

"Okay, mesh isn't the right word. But it didn't work, okay? Tell me about your day."

Gram waved at her as if she'd asked about her personal hygiene. "Same as always. But I do want more flowers. I'd like to have a garden with flowers I can pick for inside the house. It's a bit drab, don't you think?"

"Yeah. Sure." She was still in a state of surprise at the unreality of this conversation. She wasn't having to make up stuff about a ball or something and they were talking about real things like flowers.

"But about this man, you were happy. I hadn't seen you that happy since you were a child. It was nice. I'd like to see you that way more often."

"Me too, Gram. But Charlie isn't the right man for me."

"Isn't he?"

No, most definitely not.

"Did he hit you?" Gram asked quietly, her eyes focused intently on Amelia.

"No, Gram. He never laid a hand on me like that."

"So what sort of job are you going to look for next?" The abrupt change in topic was disconcerting, as Amelia was thinking of all the loving ways Charlie had touched her. But it served its purpose: getting her mind off Charlie.

That was the million-dollar question, wasn't it?

She needed to take advantage of this rare moment of lucidity from Gram, before like a fleeting memory, it disappeared.

But she couldn't think of a damn thing to talk about, put on the spot like this.

"My biggest regret of my life is that I didn't find myself in my youth. I didn't have the time with marriage and babies and avoiding Carl to discover what I wanted with my life. By the time I made the time, I was too old to do anything about it." Gram looked wistful as she spoke, staring out the window of her bedroom. Her hands relaxed in her bedspread, where they were usually clenched tightly with some unused energy.

"What did you want with your life, Gram?"

Her eyes took on a faraway sparkle. It wasn't the faraway look of Gram not being present though. The woman was all here, right now.

"I wanted experiences. Romance. Adventure. Harold was so focused on getting us things, a new car, a house with a yard, another barbecue pit. But I wanted to try escargot; I wanted to dance in the rain; I wanted to see the ocean. Grow an award-winning rose. Experiences. Not things. But I was too old for any of it by the time I realized it. That's what you should use this time for."

CHAPTER TWENTY-FOUR

Charlie carried the manila envelope through the lobby and out the door, as if it didn't cause a fiery pit of alarm to crawl around inside his belly. People didn't mail him things. Not unless it was a bill or an invitation. But his name scrawled across the front of this, no address, no return address, told him this wasn't regular mail.

Luther opened the car door for him, as usual, with his customary smile, but it faded when he saw the look on Charlie's face.

"Something up, boss?"

"Not sure, but I think so. Take the long way to Nonna's." Tonight was the first poker game with the guys. They were all supposed to be firming up plans to take down Forrester.

He was curious. Because that's who he was. A nosy motherfucker.

But this envelope was heavy in his hands, and he needed the interior of his car, a sanctuary of sorts, to look at the contents.

For the first time in weeks, he didn't think of Amelia as soon as he slid into the creamy leather seats. He didn't imagine lost moments with her in the silence of his car. Not much, anyway. He was too curious about the envelope.

He opened it, sliding the contents out. Glossy photos, still stuck together from wherever they'd been developed. Glossy photos that were only used rarely, for photo frames in family homes, and in this case, for blackmail.

Proof of something. But what? He would have to look to see.

They were dark, but the contents were clear enough. There was a picture, clearly showing Charlie's face and index finger as he beckoned someone out of his car window. Then inside his car, as he spoke to someone. Then handing them a baggie of white powder.

It was the punk, Desert Eagle, the night he'd given him the doctored drugs. Pictures showing them clearly. The kid's silver pinky ring of the skull clearly shown in the photos.

Someone was trying to blackmail him. Had a camera on the punk. He wondered if the kid had known.

Then the next picture was of something that surprised him.

Amelia.

A street view of the two of them getting in his car. Pictures of them at his desk in more intimate poses. His hand on her bare ass. His dick inside her, his hands pressing into the flesh of her hips. The look of pure ecstasy on both of their faces.

From the fucking coffee maker.

The last picture was of her in a yard, what he presumed was at her home. She was digging in the dirt, a faraway look in her eyes. He studied this picture the most, since it was the only one he hadn't been present for, yet the most threatening.

She was so sweet, flowered gardening gloves on her delicate hands. She wore jeans and a t-shirt, and sweat made her hair stick to her face around the edges. He could almost smell her sweet innocence as the picture showed her lowering a plant into the turned up dirt.

Partnership? Otherwise, next time I see her, me and the boys will see how much fun she can be …

The note was written on a piece of paper that fluttered to the floor as he stared at the last photo. He picked it up, toying with it lightly before crumpling it in his hand.

He almost laughed at the thought of blackmail. The last man who'd tried found himself at the bottom of the river. But with the pictures of the kid taken from the kid's point of view, it told him whoever was blackmailing him was the guy who was trying to undercut his contacts on the street.

The same man whom he was meeting about tonight. Forrester. Had to be. Desert Eagle had been working for him, too.

Now he was personally invested.

The pictures were meant to be scary, but Charlie smiled to himself, plotting his moves. Clearly the bug didn't have a microphone, or Forrester would be demanding more, since they'd all plotted his demise right in front of it. The pictures were a first step. He'd wait a few days for the second step: contact.

Then he'd tell Forrester to go fuck himself.

Meanwhile, he needed to keep Amelia safe, and he wasn't sure how to do that. The fact this asshole had figured out a way to take pictures of her told him she was most definitely not safe. That thought made him panic, and Charlie Delmonico didn't panic.

It was new. He needed to focus and figure out his first move.

She hated him now. Which she should, because he was a terrible human. But now she was in danger, and it was all his fault. More reasons for her to hate him. If he went to her to put a protection detail on her, which was what his first instinct was, she would only hate him more.

Charlie was pissed someone was spying, sure, but the fact they'd been privy to his more intimate scenes with Amelia was what had him seeing things through a red haze of fury.

Someone would pay for these pictures, and it wouldn't be Amelia, or him.

Luther silently watched him through the rearview mirror as he drove to the restaurant. His friend didn't say a word, understanding the mood. That was good, Charlie needed his poker face right now.

**

"Are you here for the private party with Luca?" The hostess flashed him a sweet smile as she looked up from her book at the front of the restaurant. It was full tonight; a charming din flowed around the room. He simply nodded and she led him to a room right next to where kitchen noises came from.

As he entered the room, he noticed first the hushed quiet as a contrast to the Friday evening noise in the main part of the restaurant. Then he noticed a side table filled with food and drinks. He strode over to pour himself a drink out of the bottle of scotch, then turned to the men around the table.

Mack, Luca, Dean, and Adam, all there, waiting for his arrival.

"Am I late?" His words were clipped and he mentally shook himself. His mind was still on the pictures, and he was pissed.

Someone had caught Amelia in intimate poses, her vulnerability he loved so much shining in all of them. Especially in her garden.

He didn't even know she had a garden.

Whoever had taken those pictures had stolen that knowledge from him.

"No." Adam was shuffling a deck of cards and Charlie looked on with amusement. At one point, Adam had been pretty good with them, and it seemed he still could work a mean shuffle.

Adam started dealing, laying three cards out in the middle of the table.

"Why are we here?" Mack asked pointedly as he picked up the cards Adam tossed him after laying down the river.

"I wanted to go over the order of operations, and what specifically everyone was going to do. I've been making contact with some of the officers in vice to get them on board to look the other way." He looked at Luca. "You ready to set up some poker tournaments?"

Luca smiled, looking like the boy next door. Charlie was trying to figure out how to use the kid's charm. "Yup."

Luca had been mostly a family guy since his parents had left him and his brothers with their grandma. He worked briefly for Forrester in high school, but had managed to leave the organization before getting too entrenched. That was all Charlie had been able to dig up on him after high school. A younger guy, he'd thrown himself into opening the restaurant with his grandma and siblings.

Clean cut, but with a dark side that Bascom Forrester created.

Charlie looked at his cards to see he had a bunch of shit. Nobody moved.

"I've already cloned his phone, and he's pretty obvious about his shipment times," Mack spoke up. An honorably discharged veteran, he had tons of computer skills that he'd tried to put to use in the corporate world after the Army, but he had been fired for blowing the whistle on the boss' son who he'd caught on video snorting a line of coke in the breakroom with his secretary.

He had a moral compass that could get in the way of this, but his eagerness to take down Forrester because of his sister's death seemed to overrule it.

Mack fanned his cards, straightened them back up, then fanned them out again. Charlie decided he wasn't a regular poker player, and pretty shitty too, based on how fidgety he was with his cards. Probably against his religion or some shit.

"Okay, so we'll go ahead and start on the shipment hijacking, use that for seed money for anything else we may need while we're running the poker tournies."

"You still want me to rob the banks?" Dean looked hopeful, and Charlie did not want to disappoint.

"Absolutely. We'll need those bank shares down; hopefully they'll bring down his others if we can connect the two with his name."

Dean looked relieved and Charlie felt for the guy. He was also an ex-military man who hadn't come out of the service with some fancy degree. He was currently working third shift at a warehouse for fifteen dollars an hour.

"We'll start with undermining his organization, then let Mack go in and hit his pocketbook with his little program." Mack snorted at that, but Charlie continued. "Then you can do the robberies and we'll let Adam do his thing last. It will play into the whole showdown to ruin him."

"How are we going to get the word out to the public to bring down market value?" Luca asked, even as Mack opened his mouth.

"I'll worry about that. It's sort of what I do best. Ruin images of people."

With the word images, Charlie's thoughts ran toward the pictures again. He was still pissed about that, but he was more alarmed for Amelia.

"A little off topic, but I need a favor. My assistant is no longer with me, but she needs another job. Anyone got anything?"

Adam smiled at him knowingly, but Luca spoke first. "I can always use a waitress or a bartender."

The idea of his Amelia fending off advances from drunks at a bar turned Charlie's stomach.

"I got something. I need an office worker, someone to greet off the streeters and handle deliveries and stuff." Adam spoke, and Charlie relaxed. That was much better. Hiding her out of sight of the public, and Adam would pay her better than waitressing tips.

Adam leaned back in his chair, fishing something out of his jacket pocket. "And if anyone needs to do any recon in his house, I sold Mrs. Forrester an atrocious art piece last month, and she's invited me to her annual anniversary party. I managed to make copies of the invite, if anyone wants one."

He dropped five expensive linen envelopes on the table, and Charlie grinned.

"Nice…"

Now, Luca was one he couldn't quite wrap his head around. Did he have the stomach for what they were going to do?

He'd have to find out.

CHAPTER TWENTY-FIVE

Amelia was looking for a job and gardening for Gram. That's what her life had become. A flurry of unknowns. A woman at the farmer's market had some small bushes and Amelia was planting some heirloom roses in a flowerbed Gram could see out her window. She had done her research, prepared the soil, and found a certain joy in the experience.

She was learning that gardening wasn't unknown though. The plants did exactly what you prepared for them.

She decided she loved flowers. Their sole purpose to provide beauty, in addition to oxygen. They had delicate petals in vibrant colors, the thorny stems warning away predators who might pick them and destroy the beauty. The roses turned into a sort of banner for Amelia's new life she was building for herself and Gram. She would still be a pretty flower, but she needed some sort of thorn to ward away the potential Charlies of the world, who would want to pick and destroy her.

She just didn't know what her thorn would be. She could get tattoos, but she was afraid that would keep her from getting a job, and she didn't necessarily think tattoos would deter a man of Charlie's caliber.

No, it couldn't be something physical. She needed some sort of hardened shell, and gardening in her spare time probably wouldn't grow it on her skin. But the gardening was helping her heal from the sights she'd seen, and it was available to her at this moment.

Her phone rang in the pocket of her smock. She stifled the jerk her tummy made every time it rang, schooling her voice when it wasn't Charlie.

"Hello?" It wasn't a familiar number, and with the number of applications she'd put out, she knew it had to be about a job.

"This is Beckett Art Gallery. Can you come in for an interview Tuesday at nine a.m.?" The voice sounded familiar to her and her next words were rushed.

"Yes, of course. What's the address?" She really should be asking more questions, but a job was a job, and she'd clearly talked to this guy before. Probably when she picked up an application. Or called to follow up on it. She'd been doing a lot of that too.

Although, she didn't remember an art gallery.

He gave her the address and she hung up, feeling a little giddy. She didn't even question anything about it, just knowing it was legit. She felt it in her bones.

**

Tuesday morning, she showed up at an office off a warehouse by the docks. The man who approached from the back had her picking her jaw up off the floor.

"I didn't put in an application here," she said stupidly. "Charlie told you to hire me."

Adam wore an expensive suit, and she almost walked away then. She was finished with men in expensive suits, but the smirk he sent her calmed her nerves a bit. It was a look of being in on a joke *with* her instead of making her the butt of one.

"While primarily an art gallery, this is also an import/export business. I need someone to be here during the day, answer phones, sign for deliveries, things of that ilk. I'm away from the office quite a bit, but I have been told you can be trusted with merchandise and won't ask too many questions I don't have time for. I also know for a fact, you can be professional in the face of rudeness and will make sure clients respect my time." He seemed almost bored, but the tone soothed her. She didn't want an interesting job. She had enough taking her mental capacities with Gram, and the garden was helping her emotions. She just needed money. And when he gave her a number for her paychecks, she was satisfied.

Thoughts of Charlie swam around in her head as she listened to Adam talk. They had a similarity to them, but were opposites physically. Where Charlie was a bit shorter than Adam, his muscles were bulkier. Adam was leaner. Adam's suits were lighter in color, as was his blond hair. Charlie wore dark-gray or black suits and had hair like a raven.

"Does Charlie ever come here?" She had to know if she would see him. Still torn about her past with him, she had no idea if it would ever be behind her.

She was having a difficult time breathing. Her heartbeat rushed loudly in her ears, and she realized she'd squeaked her question instead of asking it with a normal voice.

Could she work for a friend of Charlie's? She wasn't sure. She might see him, though it seemed unlikely. Was this import/export business as illegal as what Charlie did for a living? On the surface, it didn't seem so, but Amelia knew just enough about the doings of criminals to jump to dangerous conclusions, her recent binge-watching of *Criminal Minds* giving her plenty of fodder.

Still, this was the first time she'd heard Charlie Delmonico's name in weeks. It simultaneously soothed and bothered her, and she knew exactly why.

"Is he a deal breaker? I should know better. If so, I'll be sorry to lose your services. I really do need a good front-end person." Surely, he wasn't making double entendres with her?

"No, not a deal breaker. I may need some advanced warning to prepare though." She laughed through the lie, trying to reassure the man. She wanted the job, a stupid way to be closer to Charlie, even if she never saw him. He'd never lied to her. He'd told her he was a bad man.

She was the one who hadn't heeded the warning.

Maybe this wasn't a good idea. Would she constantly think about Charlie, here, in the space belonging to his friend? Would she wonder when she'd get to see Charlie again? Would she know all about the poker games and be tempted to ask questions?

"Yes, I'll take the job." She could try it anyway. What could it hurt?

"One other thing. I have an engagement next week. A client who's invited me to her anniversary party. It is only professional;

you won't have to pretend to be my date or anything." Mr. Beckett's mouth turned down in distaste. "But I loathe going to these things alone, and as my administrative assistant, it wouldn't be out of line for you to accompany me. Do you have suitable attire?"

"Yes." What was it with men not having women to go with them to functions? "As long as it's not a vaguely covered up ploy for sex, I'll go."

"There's the ballbuster I called for an interview." Adam graced her with a rare smile, and she smiled in return. Up until now, she didn't think he remembered her.

"Yes, sir."

CHAPTER TWENTY-SIX

That night, on the ride home, Charlie had given Luther the details of the new plan. He would need Luther's help, as well as his contacts to get Luca set up with some muscle for his "casino." He could also provide names for Charlie, if he knew what they were up to.

Luther had worked in Charlie's shadow for years, and he would continue to do so. Luther would have it no other way. He'd tried to bring the man in on a partner level, but he'd refused.

This morning, he ordered a new conference table. Not that his old one was in poor shape, but he wanted Forrester to be unable to resist the chance to bug his conference room.

And now he waited. He'd paid for expedited delivery and was currently researching the newspaper for reporters who seemed to be waiting for a chance to break something big. One aspect of their new plan was to take down Forrester's real estate division, drive his share prices down. The best way to do that was with some bad press.

Unfortunately, Bascom Forrester owned one of the newspapers in the city.

But Charlie thought he found something when he saw an article in the women's section on a local church organization who was working toward helping trafficking victims get back on their feet. It was written by an activist, and when he looked at her past articles, he saw tips on removing stains from silk, book reviews, and vapid things like that. It was clear she was chomping at the bit for something of substance and had probably fought tooth and nail to write this piece. The only reason she'd been able to was because of the women's church group angle.

He was supposing a lot on this assumption, but in his gut, he felt it was right.

Heidi Jones. He texted her name to Mack, telling him to look her up and make sure she was who he thought she was.

His door opened and Luca entered, poking his head around it first. Charlie waved at him to enter. Perfect timing. The new conference table he didn't need was set to be delivered any minute.

"Hey! Come on in." He gestured him to sit in the seat across from his desk.

Luca affably sauntered in and sat where Charlie gestured, relaxed yet poised.

"What's up?" Luca asked as he quirked an eyebrow.

"You got a girlfriend?"

Luca shook his head, even as his eyes shadowed with questions. Charlie got it. He was a veritable stranger, and that was a relatively personal question.

"I don't do women." Luca started to backtrack. "Okay, I do women. I don't do girlfriends."

"Why not?"

A shrug. "I've been busy. And I've never really found one that was worth it. Why?" His skeptical look told Charlie he was done answering inane questions.

He decided to be straight with the kid.

"I just can't get a read on you. That's all. You seem like you may be too good for this operation."

Luca shifted. "Look. I want to see Forrester ruined. Make no mistake about that. And if my relationship with girls is how you're going to judge my ability to take part in this, then let's just say, I have yet to spend time with a woman I haven't wanted to spank for one reason or another. They're too much of a headache."

Charlie found himself chuckling at that description.

"Yeah, I've wanted to spank a few myself." He quieted as thoughts of Amelia filled his brain.

Then the reason he'd wanted Luca here today came into the office. To Luca, he said, "Come with me."

A man muscled his enormous box inside his office, and Charlie was pleased to see it was the same pierced, tattooed douchebag who'd come before.

He strode out to meet the guy who was looking at Amelia's desk with disappointment. Luca followed.

Charlie remembered clearly how much the kid had flirted with his woman on his last visit, and it made this afternoon's potential activities that much more exciting.

"You're missing some decorations this morning, Mr. Delmonico," the cheeky bastard was saying as he leaned on his dolly, breathing hard from his exertions.

Charlie smiled in anticipation of the further exertion he was going to cause the young man. He sent Luther a text and slipped his phone in his pocket.

"I'm at a disadvantage, young man. You know my name, and I don't know yours." He kept his tone even, affable, but the tightening in his chest told him he was looking forward to extracting information from the kid. At the same time, he'd be able to find out if Luca had the stomach for this.

He held out a hand with letters on the knuckles. Classy. "Dylan Monroe. At your service." Kid was grinning like he hadn't just sealed some deal with the devil. By the end of the day, Dylan Monroe would be promising Charlie his firstborn child. A sharp intake of breath came from behind him, and Charlie wondered about Luca's reaction.

"Dylan." Charlie let the name roll over his tongue. "Let's go for a walk."

Luca followed, a few paces behind.

They rode down the elevator, with Dylan whistling over the view. "I don't get to take this elevator. It's nice. You can see everybody. And the street. Over there." He was pointing out the view, and Charlie managed to smile indulgently. "Do I know you?" He looked at Luca, and Luca shook his head, looking at his feet.

Charlie took Dylan's elbow, leading him through the lobby, and Larry noticed.

"Everything okay, Mr. Delmonico?" The security guard had stood behind his desk, his hand on the pepper spray.

"Yes, thank you. My friend and Dylan and I are just getting some air, that's all." He gave Larry a genuine smile, wishing he hadn't just drawn attention to their actions, but there was nothing to be done for it.

Outside, Luther waited with his door open, and Charlie muscled the kid inside, who was just now realizing something was wrong.

"What are you doing?" Luca had squeezed in as well and was watching silently.

"We're going to drive around and you're going to tell me how much Forrester pays you for his dirty work, and what exactly you do for him." Charlie got into the car on the other side, caging the kid in.

"What? I don't know what you're talking about."

"Luther? Would you mind driving to that old field by the airport? It's nice and quiet out there. No people, right?"

"Yes, sir." Luther was playing his part.

"Now, try again." Charlie turned back to the kid as he bent over to retrieve the baseball bat Luther had left for him inside the car.

He tapped it into his palm, making a smacking noise that had the kid flinching.

"Sir, no disrespect intended, but you remember the last Town Car we had when you talked inside of it with the baseball bat?" Luther was ridiculously good at this. Charlie looked over at Luca, whose mouth was set in a grim line of determination, his eyes hard.

He wouldn't do too badly at all this.

The tapping stopped and Charlie put on a thoughtful face. "That's right. We had to get rid of it, didn't we? You couldn't get the stains out?"

Luther nodded and Dylan paled considerably. Luca gave a soft smile, as if he were reminiscing.

"He doesn't pay me enough, obviously." He started talking. "I just deliver stuff for him, from his warehouse to wherever he tells me to." Dylan's eyes roamed to Luca's, who shook his head slightly.

Charlie filed that away. Was Luca working for Forrester still?

"I'm going to need addresses, Dylan."

Luther drove while Dylan talked. An hour later, they pulled over to the airport field Charlie had talked about. They had names, addresses, dates, and all the things they needed to get started.

"Well, you were right about one thing, Dylan." The kid looked at him hopefully. He was crying, a blubbering mess that didn't give Charlie any of the feelings Amelia's tears did. These were the tears of the weak.

"What, sir?"

"He doesn't pay you enough."

Dylan didn't see the baseball bat coming, as it crunched into his ribs.

"When this is over with, you'll be on my payroll. You'll tell Forrester you quit because you've been in a horrible car accident, making his deliveries, and then I'll have some jobs for you." The baseball bat came down on his thigh next. It would take a few months for him to heal, but after Charlie was finished with him, he would be loyal to a fault.

Because fear did that to people.

When Dylan was a crumpled, bloody mess on the field, Charlie turned to Luca, who had stood off the side, watching the whole thing.

"What the fuck was that about?" Luca asked.

"I had to see if you could take it. But now that I see you can, I'm wondering how? Mr. Clean Cut has a sense of the underworld about him." He wielded his bat, menacingly. "Do you need to have a taste to let me get a feel for you?" Charlie was bluffing, trying to see how much Luca would tell him.

Luca's chest puffed slightly as he took a step forward.

"I worked for Forrester in high school, doing what this punk does. I quit when my grandma found out. Do with that what you will." He was daring Charlie, the look in his dark eyes swirling with anger and intensity.

"Even after taking your home and leaving your Gram in a hovel?"

"Even after. He didn't leave me much choice."

"How did you just quit?"

Luca looked at Dylan. "Much the same way as your friend, here. Got the shit beat out of me and pretended to be in traction for a year until he forgot about me."

Luther came around the car.

"Get this piece of shit to the hospital and take me and Luca back to the office so he can get his car."

He had learned what he needed to. Luca would do just fine.

CHAPTER TWENTY-SEVEN

Amelia was outside, pulling dead blooms off Gram's roses after an evening of telling her of her new job in veiled terms of a consort of sorts. She explained Adam Beckett as a sponsor, who was giving her money in return for being a secretary for his secretary. It was all a bunch of nonsense, and not something she was sure ever really happened in Regency England, but whatever. It allowed her to talk to Gram without lying to her outright.

She sighed as she sat in the tilled dirt and gently picked around the thorny roses. They were looking more beautiful every day, and she got a lot of enjoyment from them.

But not enough. Even the job, which supported the both of them perfectly and didn't require much more from her than the description stated was nice. But it didn't do what it needed to for her fulfillment.

She wasn't changing anything in her world with it.

But something else had happened that she thought would, if she could get around this ever-present panic.

She dropped the dead flowers into her apron pocket and sat back on her heels.

She was pregnant.

Amelia Flores would exist as this baby's mother. It would depend on her for everything in its first years, and that was heady. Her existence was something outside of Gram, her job, and this house. It would be as a mother.

That was such an abstract thought for her, since the baby was smaller than a lima bean inside her uterus at this point. The last time she'd had this feeling, it had literally been beaten out of her.

Now she didn't quite trust it.

The father was a killer who had beaten the first baby's father to within an inch of his life, so she knew it wasn't something she could keep from him. But at the same time, did she want him in the baby's life? Really?

Something inside her that had been withering and dying the last few weeks sparked to life right then.

She'd tried her best to put Charlie out of her mind, but it had been impossible. For someone who had been a part of her life for such a short time, he'd imprinted on her in a big way.

Granted, she'd watched him for months before, fantasizing about him, daydreaming, and making up all sorts of scenarios involving him. But his reality was so much bigger, it took her breath away.

Literally. She was gasping in lungfuls of air as she sat in her garden, wishing she had a bench so she wasn't wallowing in the dirt.

Thoughts of Charlie were overwhelming. Even before she'd figured out she was pregnant, he'd overwhelmed her. She'd just tried to turn them off, but it had been impossible. Every time she drank a cup of coffee, she saw his delight at her foam pictures. Each time she dressed, she imagined him peeling off the clothes. She'd see a random smile on the street and think of his. Even getting into her car, she thought of his car and Luther's smiles in the rearview mirror.

Everything reminded her of Charlie, and each memory made her miss him terribly. It was an aching, turning of her insides, until sometimes she thought she'd spill from the inside out. It was pain. It was terror. It was everything.

And she finally thought she understood him. He thrived on these sorts of emotions, probably because he never really felt them himself. She knew he'd had some sort of awful childhood and his inability to feel fear and sadness was linked to that. Her own fear and sadness, for whatever reason had done something to him, and he'd tried to eradicate it, because that's what he did.

He was a fixer.

Whatever black heart he'd had was in the right place. Even as she thought that, she knew Charlie wasn't as bad as he said he was.

He loved her. And he would love a child. She didn't doubt that at all.

He would do everything he could to be a father to the child.

Her hand drifted absently to her belly, wondering how long it would take to feel it kick. Start showing? Feel morning sickness?

And she didn't really want to do it alone.

Logistics aside, she had to tell him. She didn't know anything about the details of co-parenting, and everything she knew about Charlie told her the books and articles wouldn't shed any light on it. Not with him.

CHAPTER TWENTY-EIGHT

"Destiny?" Charlie's smooth voice spoke out his lowered window to the woman standing outside her building, next to her doorman as she chatted idly. She nodded and got into the car next to him, overwhelming him with the scent of expensive perfume.

"Mr. Delmonico, right?" He nodded.

"Charlie, tonight." She was pretty, in a purposeful, made-up way. A stark contrast to Amelia's beauty, she had long blond hair, long legs, and wore a dress that was too short. It was a metallic gold color, and her makeup was fixed artfully, while her hair hung in a long sheet down her back. Her shoes were also gold and high.

"It's nice to meet you." He could hear Luther's grunt from the front seat and knew his friend was mad at him. He'd filled Luther in on everything, and Luther had argued about hiring a woman for tonight's party.

The truth was, Luther had been right, and Charlie knew it. Tonight wouldn't go as well with Destiny on his arm, but he hated these events by himself. Single men stuck out like a sore thumb, and he needed to not stick out. He was there to make a statement, and that was all.

"Tonight won't last long. I need to appear at this function just long enough for an important person to see me, then we'll leave. You are my date, and if you see someone you know, please be subtle about it. You're supposed to be with me," he told the woman more as a reminder than anything else. "If it works out, there may be more functions in the future."

"Don't worry. If I see someone I know, they won't want me to acknowledge them." She grinned at him, and he relaxed somewhat.

Hiring a woman always had its drawbacks, but the service he used was expensive, and it was because of their discretion.

**

Amelia wore her favorite little black dress from her shopping spree with Charlie's money. It was simple, yet elegant, and she wore her grandma's pearls with it. She felt like Jackie Kennedy, walking up to the door of the house on Adam's arm. He had loosened up a little bit since she'd started working for him, even if he was still really uptight.

The house was gorgeous. Massive on the outside, the inside was tastefully decorated in soft golds and reds, exuding money as if it would start falling from the ceiling at any moment. Furniture had been moved out to make room for hundreds of people who spilled into rooms that were surely formal living and dining areas.

Adam shook the hand of a man and woman at the door greeting guests.

"Adam Beckett!" The woman leaned in to kiss him on both cheeks, something affected by the European from generations of habit, or the rich, from decades of posing. It was hard to tell without knowing the woman. "Bascom, Adam is the one who acquired that lovely cherub in the outer courtyard for me. And he's going to get me more pieces. Remember?"

Bascom Forrester grunted as he held his hand out, but he was staring at Amelia. Her skin prickled under his gaze as he reached for her.

"And who is this lovely creature?" She had let him clasp her hand in his, and he was kissing the knuckles, his grip loose and cold. His lips left a glossy patch on her hand, and she resented it. She didn't like random men's lips on her skin.

"This is my assistant, Amelia. I thought your lovely wife may want to meet the woman who does all the grunt work at my office. Without her, I may not be able to get everything done in a timely manner."

All the fake sweetness was giving Amelia a cavity. Meanwhile, Bascom stared at her through lowered lids, as if he had X-ray vision. It was creepy.

The wife gushed. "Oh my! Well, help yourselves to anything. And if you need something special to drink, just ask Edward. He's floating around here somewhere."

Amelia might. She wondered what sort of non-alcoholic options were available, but she wasn't about to search out some guy named Edward. Surely, they had club soda.

As they made their way into the room, Amelia realized how tense Adam had been. His arm relaxed under her hand and she squeezed, acknowledging his relaxation. She could only wish she felt the same. Her own stomach was twisting uncomfortably.

He leaned down and whispered in her ear. "Just pretend it's all yours." Was she tense? Acting weird?

She pasted a smile on her face, and replied, "I can't. I would never paint the walls this color." He barked out a laugh and patted her hand, leading her to the end of the room where they could watch people.

For what, she had no idea, but if she knew anything about her boss, it was that he was careful. He wasn't the type to run the world from a stage. He was a behind-the-curtain kind of guy, like Charlie, pulling levers and drawing strings to manipulate things to his desires.

It was as if she manifested him out of thin air. As soon as she thought it, Charlie came in the door, shaking hands with the couple greeting guests. Bascom smiled and said something to him. Charlie's face morphed into cheeks turned red, deep crimson slashes that made a stark contrast to his tan skin, and his head swung toward her immediately, his eyes locking on hers.

All of the air suddenly evaporated from the room, and no one else existed. The chatter around them dimmed to a muffled buzz, and everything in Amelia's peripheral vision faded away.

Her stomach's twisting intensified as she fell into the abyss of Charlie's eyes. She'd never seen him look so surprised, and then angry, as his eyes shifted to Adam next to her, then her hand on his arm.

But that wasn't all. As Amelia drank him in, an elegant, manicured hand stroked his chest. The hand was connected to a leggy supermodel, and Amelia's heart exploded into a million pieces. He had his arm around her waist, like he'd done with Amelia on several occasions.

She knew what the woman was. And she knew if she hadn't left him, that would be Amelia stroking Charlie's chest like she owned him. But it still didn't help.

"You didn't tell me Charlie would be here," she whispered out of the side of her mouth to Adam.

"I didn't know it would matter."

"It wouldn't have. But I asked for a warning, didn't I?"

She suddenly felt sick. She wasn't ready to talk to him. It was something she knew she had to do, but this wasn't the right place, and certainly not the right time.

"I'm going to go find a restroom. I'll be right back," she muttered before making short work of getting the hell out of the same room as Charlie Delmonico.

There was a long hallway off the living area, doors open to showcase more rooms with walls covered in artwork. There was a study, a movie theater, and a small sitting room, but no restroom. Her desperation grew bigger with each room that wasn't a restroom with a locking door. Spying Edward, she asked him, "Is there a restroom?"

"Of course. There is one on the other side of the living room." Edward must have seen her pale features and the look of mortification on her face at the daunting task of going back through the living room with Charlie in it. "The closest one is in the garage, though. Through the kitchen, if you'll excuse it not being really set up for guests."

"Thank you." She spun around and flew through the kitchen doors, her stomach heaving. She swallowed hard and darted around the staff and caterers working to go out the door to the outside and follow a small breezeway to the garage.

Leaning over the sink, she took in great lungfuls of air, wanting her stomach to settle. She swallowed down the bile that had risen in her throat, willing it back to her stomach where it belonged. She gulped a time or two, then looked at herself in the mirror.

Deciding it wasn't too bad, she got a towel, wet the corner, and swiped it across the back of her neck.

She knew she'd run across him at some point. He worked with Adam. Or Adam worked with him. Whatever. But they were associates of some sort, and she was a smart girl. They apparently ran in the same circles, and she would see him.

Amelia just hadn't been expecting it to be tonight. So soon.

She laughed at herself. It wasn't soon. She was just a chickenshit.

Things would never be right between them again. Baby or no baby. He would go home and fuck his date for the evening, and she would go home to Gram.

She exhaled a breath, finally feeling more composed and straightened herself. This room was bigger than she realized at first, probably as large as her own kitchen, which was a stupid waste for a bathroom in the garage.

Amelia took a deep breath and exhaled hard. She had to be a grown-ass woman about all this. She was here in a professional capacity. Charlie was a part of her past. Sure, seeing him hurt, but it was for the best. She couldn't be with him, knowing that he would hurt people on her behalf without listening to her first.

Was that what this was? Was she pissed about that?

Oh God. She had to think about that another time. She really needed to get back to the party, and not give Adam a reason to fire her.

Quietly, she let herself out the door and into the garage. She hadn't noticed the cars in there before, on her single-minded mission to get to a bathroom. But she saw them now, as well as the empty bays.

Bascom Forrester, the man who owned the house, was standing in the middle of a semi-circle of men, all looking at her hungrily.

"I see Mr. Delmonico sweetened the terms of our deal." His eyes crawled down her body as he leered at her, taking a step toward her. There were so many things she could say, should say, but the look in his eyes stole her words. She was suddenly more scared than she'd ever been in her life.

She took a step backward and felt the hard muscle of another man as his arms came up and clamped around her chest.

She was in trouble.

CHAPTER TWENTY-NINE

Charlie had shaken Forrester's hand absently, as his wife spoke to his date about drinks and some guy named Edward. But he couldn't stop looking at Amelia.

Focus.

She was gorgeous tonight. She glowed, even if she did look a little green at the sight of him. Her eyes, dark-brown pools of the darkest chocolate, her pale skin, her ebony hair. She was fucking exquisite. And she had a death grip on Adam.

Fucking Adam.

As soon as she left the room, Charlie strode over to Adam.

"Why did you bring her here?" This place would taint her. Forrester lived here, propped his feet up here, fucked his wife here. If Bascom Forrester was as horrible a person as these guys thought he was, why would he bring someone as innocent and good as Amelia into the lion's den?

"I needed a date." Adam's shrug infuriated him.

"You should have rented one, like I did." Charlie jerked his chin at Destiny, who was making her way over to them. She casually twined her arm through Charlie's, and he shrugged her off. "Where did she go?" he demanded. His intention was to get her out of here, but the way she looked, he'd have a hard time keeping his hands off her.

He could pass Destiny off to Adam, and then take Amelia home. It was a long enough drive; maybe he could talk to her on the way.

Yeah, he needed to talk to her.

"Said she needed to go to the bathroom. I'm her boss, not her keeper," Adam said, his shoulders stiffening under his expensive suit. It was a nice suit. Charlie had one just like it at home.

Charlie had done what he needed to do. He'd given Forrester his best fuck-off vibe, let him know he knew where he lived by showing up at his wife's party uninvited, and now he could go.

But he wasn't leaving without Amelia. The need to see her hadn't been so strong until he'd seen her.

That didn't mean he'd managed to get her out of his head. Nope. She was always there, but like a curtain that shrouded everything. She was a filter to his life, once giving it color, but now that she was gone, the color was dampened.

It sucked.

He wanted her back, but he knew he didn't deserve her. At any rate, when he'd told Adam to give her a job, this wasn't what he'd meant. She was supposed to sign for shit, not attend parties.

He looked at Destiny. "Change of plans. You're his date tonight." Amelia being here made those pictures come into focus in his brain. Forrester already knew about her, and had probably recognized her when she'd waltzed in here on Adam's arm.

Goddammit. He should have shown Adam the pictures, let him know the danger from Forrester. If he had, she wouldn't be here now.

Then he went to find Amelia. Looking around the room, there was a hallway that looked like it might have a bathroom. He opened every door, seeing lots of people mingling, but no Amelia.

A man came up behind him, dressed in a tux. "Can I help you find something, sir?"

"Yes, a woman in a black dress, she was just here. I'm looking for her. Tiny thing, short dark hair." Charlie decided this was the butler or whatever Forrester had at this party to make himself feel important.

"I believe she was feeling ill. I directed her to the garage bathroom." Pointing, he spoke with an affected accent, and Charlie briefly wondered if he learned to speak that way in butler school or whatever. But he didn't ask. He walked as quickly as he could through the kitchen and out to the garage.

When Charlie opened the door, he saw more than he'd anticipated, and the Amelia filter that dampened all the colors suddenly blinded him with a red haze of anger.

One of Forrester's goons held her while Bascom and another man were palming her bare breast. Her skirt had been hiked up around her waist. Half a dozen men stood around palming erections behind pants, or stroking their dirty dicks as they looked on. But that wasn't the worst part of it all.

No. The worst part were the tears that streaked down Amelia's face as she was limp in the man's arms.

Tears of humiliation. He'd seen them enough on others to recognize them. Helplessness, despair, fear.

Forrester made his girl feel those things, and she was too good to ever feel that way.

Feeling woefully underprepared, Charlie did what he could. He pulled his gun from the holster under his jacket and trained it on the man holding Amelia, cocking it.

The douchebag holding Amelia heard the metallic snick over the grunts and cries of encouragement and released her immediately. Smart man.

Amelia saw Charlie and ran over to him, stumbling and then kicking off her shoes. She reached him and he rested an arm on her shoulders, even as he swiveled his gun to aim at Forrester.

"I'm not going to shoot you now." His voice was cold, and everyone was suddenly silent with his words. "I'm going to let you live so you can experience what I've got in store for you." He wanted to shoot the motherfucker for making his girl cry, for hurting her, for scaring her, for even thinking about laying a hand on her. "You ever touch her again, and I will kill you. No choices. No games. You will die."

With that, he uncocked his gun and put it back in his holster, flopping his jacket over it. Forrester simply watched, his arms crossed. The other men had put away their cocks and were standing behind Forrester, waiting for his order to rip Charlie to shreds. But it wouldn't come. He had a houseful of people inside, the party his wife had planned, and appearances were too important for Bascom Forrester.

Wrapping an arm around Amelia's shoulders, he led her outside, while texting Luther on his phone to bring the car.

Death was too fucking good. Was it really? If Forrester was dead, he would be done with this shit.

Amelia's trembling body broke into his thoughts, and he stopped and wrapped his jacket around her, kissing her forehead.

"Was that the right thing?" He still wanted to kill him, but she didn't like that, did she?

She looked up at him, her deep brown eyes swimming with emotion as she stared at him. With a glazed look on her face, she nodded, and he scooped her into his arms.

Yeah, he'd ignored her with Jackson, and he'd lost her then. If he ignored her again, there was no hope for getting her back.

Not that there was, anyway, but it would be gone like ash in the wind if he didn't get a handle on things.

It didn't take long for Luther to pull the car up, but in that few minutes, Charlie held her in his arms, his mouth on the top of her head, reminding himself of her scent, why he had to let her go.

"Miss Flores, so glad to see you again." Luther's voice was loud in the night, and Charlie welcomed the sense of normalcy in his suddenly topsy-turvy night. He'd expected to see Forrester, tell him there would be no blackmail, and make his way out with some threats. Adam was supposed to be there to do more of the same, but he'd brought fucking Amelia and things had changed.

Because that's what she did. She changed everything.

They got in the car, and Amelia immediately crawled over to his side of the back seat, seeking out his comfort. Goddammit, that man had almost broken her.

He could see why all the other guys hated him so much. Charlie suddenly had a vested interest in Forrester's downfall.

"I can't change." He heard the words in the silence of the car and felt her body as she shifted to look up at him. But he couldn't look back at those eyes that saw so much. He continued looking at the back of Luther's head, his eyes focused on the road completely, but he knew his friend was listening intently. No worries. He wasn't going to tell her anything Luther didn't already know.

"I never knew my dad, and Mom died when I was young, so the loving state system took me in. Foster parents are awful. Some of them mean well; they want to mold children and teach them and make an impact on them. I had eight or nine sets of foster parents, and the first ones were the only ones like that. The rest of them taught me everything I needed to know to be successful in the life I have now. They taught me that there are always ways to make money; there are always people who have less power than you, and there are bonds that tie people together, whether advertently, like Luther here, or inadvertently, like Forrester." He jerked his chin toward the direction they'd just come from. "And that the past is just that. The past. A memory. You don't have to hold on to it and make it change you. You can just make it something that happened to you and move on."

The next words got stuck on his tongue, choking him. He needed to tell her that she was like Luther to him. A piece of his past he clung to like life. She was more than a memory; she was inside him. But he didn't. Instead, he gripped her to his body, feeling her lush curves melt into him.

She was fucking perfect.

Her finger traced his chin, and her mouth moved against his chest. Luther, who was watching in the rearview mirror, widened his eyes.

He looked down at her. "What?"

She'd said something, and he'd missed it. Luther had it though, and the knowledge that Luther knew something about this woman that he didn't peeved him. He needed her to repeat it.

"I'm pregnant."

Charlie's insides plummeted, leaving him breathless. Then they swelled, bigger than a fucking elephant. A humming started up in his ears, and Amelia's scent invaded him. Suddenly, there was nothing but the two of them, alone, together, in this car. The sounds of the tires over the highway made a rhythmic thumping noise, but he was aware of the two of them only.

His thoughts raced around in his head, but they would only settle on one thing: A picture of Amelia, fat with his child.

Minutes passed in silence, and Charlie struggled to find the right words. He couldn't. Instead, he found her hand, clutching his sleeve tightly, and twined his fingers with hers, raising it to kiss the knuckles.

She was making him a father.

That should be fucking terrifying. But it wasn't.

"I was on birth control." He knew that. He'd seen her take the pills, seen the odd little package on the bathroom countertop in Cayman.

"I know." This should change everything. She should be taking her in his lap and kissing her, letting her know he would be there for them.

But it didn't. It couldn't. He wasn't father material, not any more than some guy who got a monthly check to care for disadvantaged kids that weren't his.

But it was Amelia having his child.

“I don’t want anything from you. I just thought you would want to know.” Her voice was quiet in the interior of the car, and he wished Luther would fucking drive faster.

“I know.” He was a broken record, but he didn’t think she was a gold digger or anything. There was no way Amelia was trying to trap him into fatherhood for the child support. She wasn’t that kind of woman.

When Luther finally pulled up in front of Amelia’s house, Charlie got out with her. Leaning down, he told Luther to grab a hotel for the night, and then he followed Amelia up the steps.

She went inside and did her nightly ritual of checking on Gram, who was sleeping, and telling the nurse goodbye. Then she turned to Charlie.

“You want some water? I don’t really have anything else.” She shrugged, not having questioned his choice to spend the night with her. He shook his head.

She led the way onto the back porch, small, like everything else at this house, and sat in a rocking chair, waving him into the other one. She flipped a switch nearby, and the yard burst into dim lights around. He took in the sight and sighed.

She had created a flower garden out here. It was tiny, but in the light, he could see little bursts of flowers everywhere.

She had created this beauty. Like she would create a life.

They had created a life.

“It’s a lot to take in, I know. We weren’t together that long, and in that short amount of time, we made a new life. It’s crazy how that works.”

All of the emotion in her voice tugged at something inside him.

“I didn’t get to finish. In the car,” he started, determined to tell her everything about him. “Luther and Adam are pieces of my past, the pieces I can’t shake, but I don’t want to. They are a piece of me that’s important. The only ones that I kept in touch with, that remind me where I came from. The only piece of my past that still matters to me.” He swallowed thickly, his eyes boring into hers. “Until you. Now I can finally see a future.”

She was staring at him now. “You have done something to me, Amelia, something I can’t explain. And even before the baby, I knew I would never be able to forget you. I have no idea what sort of a person I can be for you, what sort of father to this baby I can be."

He took a deep breath and let it out slowly. "Part of me wants to hate you, because that would be so much easier, but like everything else about you, there is nothing easy about you. I can't hate you. I can't put you in my past. I can't forget you. And I can't excise you from my life completely. When you told me you loved me, I realized that I love you too." She inhaled a sharp breath, but didn't speak. "I never wanted to. Never wanted another person in my life I had to think about, certainly not before I considered myself." She heard the formality of his words and knew it was a defense mechanism. "But loving you did something to me. Changed me a little. Or at least, made me want to change for you. But I can't. All that with Jackson—" The bastard's name still tasted sour. "All that made me realize I can't change and be what you need me to be."

CHAPTER THIRTY

He was rejecting her again. He'd been fighting her from the beginning, in his own way. Scaring her with sex, beating her ex, trying to push her away. But the more he talked, the more she realized he wanted her just as badly as she wanted him.

He loved her too. She'd heard those words and discounted the rest.

"So just to clarify, you're telling me what I want? What I need?" Her voice rose toward the end, and she swallowed to shush herself. She didn't want to wake Gram.

He nodded, his eyes never leaving hers. "When I found you tonight, something snapped."

"But you reined it in." She'd seen his posture change as soon as she touched him.

He sighed, more of a groan, but didn't contradict her. "Okay, what do you want? The ball's in your court. Tell me what you want and need."

She shook her head at this stupid man who had all the power and didn't even realize it.

"I want you, Charlie. You're not a bad man. You just do things that others wouldn't, but you do it for a purpose that's beyond you. I love that. You were protecting me with Jackson, and tonight, you were protecting me from that man. I know that you would do anything to protect your child."

"So what does that mean?"

"It means I love you. The good and the bad. I want to have this child with you. I want to live with you and raise a family." She hadn't thought out the logistics, because she hadn't allowed herself to think that far ahead, but she knew that she wanted Charlie in her life, however he would be.

"You want a picket fence and a dog? I'm not that guy, Amelia." His frustration was showing and she held up her hand.

"I didn't say that. I don't want a picket fence, although with a baby, I think some redecorating may be in order."

"What about Gram?"

She shrugged. "I don't have all the answers. But together, we can come up with them." She bit her lip and waited for a response from him. He'd taken a long time to talk tonight, spending an eon thinking about what he said before he said it. It had made her crazy in the car, and she kept interrupting his thoughts with things she'd wanted to say. But now that she knew he wanted her too, loved her even, she was getting frustrated herself. "You don't have to be with me, but I want you in this baby's life, if you'll have us. I don't think you want to toss us to the side, no matter what you tell yourself I need."

It was as if her words broke something inside him. His motionless figure suddenly sprang into action. He lifted her into his arms and cradled her against his chest as if she weighed nothing, walking her into the house, down the short hallway to her bedroom.

"Gram," she reminded him, having no doubt where his mind was.

"Then be silent."

As if she could. He laid her down on the bed, before standing straight and shucking his clothing. His ritual was the same, but faster. Jacket, cufflinks, cuff buttons, then the routine changed, until he was gloriously naked in front of her.

Amelia's insides were on fire. He'd said all the right things, had all the right concerns, and was standing in front of her in her bedroom, looking sinfully … *right.*

Could she do this with him? She'd missed him so much during their time apart, and had forgiven him for the whole Jackson thing.

Was she ready to go back to the way they'd been?

Charlie looked at her with possession in his eyes, his cock rock-hard. For her. She knew all she had to do was say the word and he would call Luther and go home.

But then she would for sure never see him again. She definitely did not want to go back to the way things had been this past month.

Even thinking about that possibility made her heart beat with a despair and her stomach clench painfully.

No, she couldn't live without him.

Charlie leaned on his arms and started crawling up her body, but she stopped him with a hand to his chest. The hurt and doubt that shadowed his eyes was immediate.

"I'm sorry."

"No, I want this. But I want you to promise me something first."

He swallowed thickly, then a resolve filled his features and he lifted his chin. "I'll try."

She knew he would.

"I want experiences with you. Not stuff. I don't want the big house in the suburbs. I want to die knowing that I'd done it all. I don't want to have it all. I want to love hard, Charlie. Do that with me."

His mouth claimed hers in a kiss that held so much passion and feeling she was breathless. His tongue claimed hers, and the kiss was so hard and sudden their teeth clanged together. But she didn't care. The feel of his body, hot and hard, on top of hers was almost too much.

He took care in undressing her. Unzipping the side of her dress, and helping her shimmy out of it, without ever getting completely off her or breaking the kiss. His massive hands were everywhere, and the heated smoothness of his grip on her body was delicious and dragged her deeper into this experience.

When he broke the kiss, he buried his face in her neck, sucking hard before swiping his tongue over the mark he for sure left. Then he went lower, dragging her bra straps down as he did. He unclasped the front clasp of her bra, and her tits sprang free. He made an appreciative moan in the back of his throat, before taking one in his mouth.

"Oh God," she cried out, and his eyes immediately got mischievous. He released her breast and moved lower, slowly and gently taking her panties off.

"You can't be quiet, can you?"

"I can try." She gasped, realizing she had been a little loud.

"That's not good enough, I'm afraid. We don't want to disturb Gram." Then he stuffed her panties in her mouth and gave her a satisfied grin.

He hadn't tied her hands or restrained her at all, but she didn't want to remove the panties. He was right, she did need to be quiet, but it was something else.

Dirty.

Taboo.

What he wanted.

She gripped his hair and tugged him back up to her breast, and he obliged, spending a considerable amount of time with them, working her into a frenzy before he looked up at her.

"I need you so badly. I've missed you." The honest urgency in his eyes was something she'd never seen before, and he'd wanted her plenty. She remembered the Caymans, his office, his apartment. This was different though, and she saw the intensity and it took her breath away.

"Then take me," she mumbled around the panties in her mouth. She wasn't sure if he understood her or not, but he nodded and entered her in one swift thrust.

He lowered his head to her neck and stilled, panting hard with what seemed like restraint.

Then with a muttered curse, he wrapped his arms around her body, holding her shoulders from behind, and started moving.

His lurches against her were hard, insistent, and his hands pushed her down with every one of his thrusts. It was hard, it was fast, and her headboard groaned and squeaked in protest.

But it felt amazing.

She was gasping and moaning, but everything was muffled around the panties stuffed in her mouth. He'd been thinking on his toes with that one.

But he wasn't being all that quiet. He was cursing under his breath, the groans of "Christ" and "Fucking hell" getting louder and louder.

She was feeling it too. Amelia was clenching against the building heat inside, afraid if she came as hard as it seemed like she was going to, her gram would hear it no matter what she had stuffed in her mouth.

But the orgasm barreled down on her, and even as Charlie moved in and out, banging her bed around in the tiny room, everything inside her tightened up with a burning intensity and the heat pooled outward, making every single limb convulse with sensation.

Charlie froze, pulling her down by the shoulders as he pulsed up with his cock, and he sucked the skin of her shoulder into his mouth, biting it with a groan.

It hurt, but it was wonderful, and she wanted to do it again and again and again.

And as soon as they recovered, they did.

CHAPTER THIRTY-ONE

Amelia had stayed silent about whatever secret place Charlie was taking her to. When she'd asked, he'd simply told her curiosity killed the cat, and given her a funny look. She could tell whatever he was about to expose her to was important to him, and not many people knew about it.

She could appreciate that, as well as his effort.

He was stiff and quiet on the drive there, and even Luther kept his eyes to himself, not looking back at them once.

But she couldn't resist scooching over to his side of the car and wrapping her arm around his middle and resting her head on him.

He reciprocated with a heavy sigh, putting his arm around her.

"This reminds me of the first time you rode in this car with me," he murmured onto the top of her head.

She looked up at him and saw a soft smile curving the edges of his lips.

"I had the most inappropriate thoughts that night."

"I was sleeping in your lap," she reminded him, remembering her own embarrassment at her drool.

"One of these days I'll let you in on my train of thought that night, and maybe we can fulfill a fantasy of mine."

She grinned at him saucily, feeling a little tug of playfulness. She'd gotten the impression he wasn't really in a playful mood, but she wanted him to tell her his fantasies. She wanted to fulfill them for him.

When the car stopped, she was surprised to see a cemetery on the edge of a large pocket of woods.

Amelia looked at Charlie, nothing but questions bouncing around her brain.

"I wanted to introduce you to my mother." Then he opened the car and got out, holding his hand to help her out of the car.

It had been two weeks since they'd gotten back together. In that time, they'd split their time between his apartment and Gram's house. They still didn't have the answers about where they would live permanently, but things seemed to be working themselves out. Luther took her to Adam's warehouse office, then took Charlie to work, and picked her up at quitting time. Charlie even came by for lunch about twice a week.

And there was lots of sex. Every night. Every morning. And sometimes at lunch.

She blamed pregnancy hormones. Something about an increased blood flow to her nether regions. She was always swollen and ready for him.

But not now. Well, she was ready for him physically, because it was a physiological response. But mentally, she was in a cemetery, about to see where Charlie's mother was buried. So no. She wasn't getting ready to drop her pants and let him have his way with her.

He led her to the outskirts of the graves and sat her in a bench that faced the trees, her back to the headstones. It was a weird placement, but she didn't question it, as Charlie seemed to be working out of habit.

She imagined the names on the headstones and how they marked places for loved ones to visit. Since she and Charlie had been back together, she hadn't had many more existential crises, but there had been the stray, "What will happen when I die; who will I be then; who will remember me?" thoughts in the middle of the night, like always.

And then she'd turn and snuggle into Charlie, and they'd stop.

He clutched her hand as they settled into the bench, and she looked at him. His strong jaw was clenched, his brows scrunched down over his eyes. He wasn't wearing a suit today, but had on jeans and a hoodie, and if she hadn't known it was her Charlie, she probably wouldn't have recognized him.

They had spent some casual time together the last couple of weeks, but even casual, he still seemed more dressed up than most. This was the most casual she'd ever seen him.

And his eyes were watering.

"Are you okay?"

He was still staring into the trees.

"Talk to me. You're scaring me." She'd never seen him like this, not since the night of the party. He looked so frazzled, like he was falling apart.

"When I was fourteen, my mom disappeared." He began, his voice sounding thick and a bit choked. "The cops thought she had gone back to her old ways and didn't pay much attention to her disappearance." Charlie looked over at her, then down at their still clasped hands. "She'd been in trouble with the law when I was little—drugs. But she'd cleaned up and had a hair studio in our garage. We didn't have a lot, but we had each other. It wasn't drugs that made her disappear and I knew it. Since she'd gotten clean when I was around eight, she'd been both a mother and a father to me, since my dad was unknown."

"I'm so sorry." And she meant it. What would it have been like to lose her mother at such a young age? To not have anybody?

"Yeah, well, it wasn't until some guy walking his dog out here found my mom's skull in those woods that they realized something had happened to her. It was bashed in. Her clothes were stuffed in a tree trunk. They never found all of her. I never got to bury all of her. Any of her really. Some forensics lab somewhere has what's left of her in case they get a suspect."

"So they don't even have a clue who did it?"

He shook his head.

"I can make a ton of excuses, saying this is why I am the way I am, but the truth is I've learned to be the way I am, because this is how I've needed to be my whole life." Charlie finally turned to look at her. "Does that make sense?"

"I wouldn't have you any other way, Charlie. I'm sorry that this has happened to make you this way, but I'm not sure I would love you the same way if you were different." It was the truth too. If he didn't have the darkness inside him, would she have ever seen it and been attracted to him?

"I brought you out here for a reason." Charlie took both her hands in his and then dropped to the ground between her knees. "I'm at your mercy, and probably have been since the first moment I laid eyes on you. I don't know what our future holds, but I know that I can't live it without you. I don't think Gram will like my apartment, and I don't think I can stuff panties in your mouth every time we fuck. So I want us to all get another place together, and I also know that Gram wouldn't appreciate it if we lived in sin. So make an honest man out of me, Amelia. I love you. Marry me."

"I love you too." She reached out and stroked his cheek, the thick stubble on his cheek testament to the fact he hadn't shaved this morning. "Of course I'll marry you."

He smiled, and as tired as he seemed after baring his mother's story to her, it dropped ten years off his face. Then he stood, spun around to the trees, and yelled, "She said yes!"

Of course, if some of his mother's bones were in a lab somewhere, that meant the rest were here. He'd just proposed in front of his family.

The car horn honked short staccato bursts to the tune of "Shave and a Haircut," showing that Luther had heard too.

Amelia laughed, and Charlie scooped her into his arms.

"Take me home and tell me about this fantasy in your car…" she muttered against his lips as he kissed her.

EPILOGUE

2 months later…

Charlie gripped Amelia's thighs on either side of his hips as she moved on top of him. He loved watching her like this, free and uninhibited. She had gotten so much more comfortable with herself and freer than he'd ever imagined with her body. He watched her climax as her fingernails dug into his chest and scraped long gashes of his skin, felt her grip him with her insides, before grabbing her hips and holding her still so he could pound up into her for his own release.

She collapsed on top of him, her breasts pressing into his chest, both of them heaving ragged gulps of air.

"I love you, Charlie."

"I love you too." His voice was hoarse with emotion, but it could be the exertion. At any rate, it still brought him to his proverbial knees when she said those words. He would never tire of hearing them. "Speaking of which, would you still love me if I had to use a cane?"

Amelia lifted her head and stared at him with one eyebrow crooked. "What do you have up your sleeve now, meddler?"

"Oh, you know me, always plotting and planning something."

Charlie rolled her off him and got out of bed. Stretching, he spotted a pair of pajama pants on the floor and put them on before going into the kitchen to make some coffee.

Gram was there already, wearing a housecoat that buttoned up to her neck and pouring two cups of coffee for them. She already had a cup with a tea bag dangling out of it.

"I know this isn't up to Amelia's standard, but I'm trying to make myself useful. And make some noise."

Heat rose to Charlie's face. He'd tried to make adjustments to his lifestyle out of respect for the old woman suddenly living with him, but she seemed to take it all in stride.

"Will you be here for supper tonight?" Gram asked. She'd been doing much better here. He had Nancy coming in to stay with her during the day, and her lucid days were more and more frequent. He didn't have nearly as many pickles as he'd expected.

"I will be here for supper, but I can bring takeout so nobody has to cook. Also, I'm leaving for a week tomorrow, so you won't have to worry about me for a little while." He grinned before taking a sip of his coffee, stifling a grimace.

Lucid or not, she couldn't make a cup of coffee to save her soul.

He would need to find a bigger house for them all, but things seemed to be working out anyway. Charlie looked forward to his future, and he couldn't remember when that had been a thing in his life.

***

Bascom Forrester held his glass of scotch, swirling it around, watching the legs as they trickled down the sides of the glass.

He'd spent years building this empire of his, ever since his father had insisted hard work was the only way to have it. Bascom had proved him wrong by taking over his real estate firm when he wouldn't give it to him. Hostile takeovers were a lot of work though, and it hadn't taken him long to realize he could buy what he wanted instead.

In the form of gangs, intimidation, and of course, selling illicit materials on the side, he'd managed to build up a rather large kingdom.

He smiled to himself. It was like an alternate reality just under the surface of everyone else's world. His brother ruled the law-abiding one, from his perch in the police station, but he helped Bascom with his own lawless domain, by turning a blind eye to his actions.

But this Charlie Delmonico character was a force. He couldn't figure the man out; he didn't seem to want in on his dealings personally. Except that woman. He'd almost cracked the man with that. Bascom had done research on the man. He was a fixer and didn't do stuff for personal glory.

Pussy.

No. He did shit for money, which wasn't unadmirable, but was certainly not as passionate as Bascom.

"Hey, brother. Got another one of those?" He looked up to see Bentley standing at the doorway. His brother was older by three years, but looked younger, dammit. Trimmer, his hair had stayed salt and pepper, instead of the silver that his own had. His paunch was smaller, he was taller, and by comparison, Bascom looked … old.

He sighed. "Help yourself," he said, gesturing toward the bar in the corner.

"How are the shipments?"

"One was hijacked last night." Bascom wondered if Charlie had anything to do with that. He used truckers, always had. They were good for a lot of things: drugs, guns, women, fenced goods. Nobody looked twice at them. Freight trucks were everywhere.

He couldn't exactly report the hijackings.

"I'll look into it. What was it?"

"Just grass. Not as much money as other stuff."

"You sound like a fucking hippie when you call it that."

"Dope?"

His brother shook his head at him, smiling ruefully before gulping his drink down. "I was just coming in to check on you."

"Check on Charlie Delmonico, why don't you? I'm fine. I think Charlie's making trouble." He had royally pissed the guy off by messing with his woman.

Why men let women hold on to their junk so hard, Bascom would never understand. They were a means to an end, a warm hole to find pleasure in, but never, ever one to hold your testicles in their purse.

Charlie had shown his hand by letting that little pixy hold his.

Bascom wasn't done. Not by a long shot.

***

The next week...

"I'm going to get some wood. If I'm not back in ten minutes, come after me." Charlie seemed to be joking, but the guys had been making jokes about wild animals in this wilderness for so long, the jokes had lost their humor.

Luca could only nod his agreement.

He was hot, dirty, and really fucking tired. He'd been following Mack and Charlie for two days, through the woods, across a river, under barbed wire, and up at least two fucking walls.

Team building my ass.

This was torture, pure and simple.

Luca wasn't a metrosexual, by any stretch of the imagination, but this shit was for cavemen and barbarians. If he had to eat another MRE in his life, he would just shoot himself. Bland, tasteless packets of starch was what those were.

When Charlie had first come to them with the idea that they needed to work as a unit to take Bascom Forrester down, therefore, they needed to become a brotherhood, Luca had imagined a camping trip, with fireside cooking, fishing, and drinking.

Not some Crucible-type thing that Mack and Dean had dreamed up from their service days.

They'd been at this for forty-eight hours, with no end in sight.

Luca was ready for his bed, and really wasn't having brotherly thoughts about any of these men.

It was Charlie's idea, so he was the most gung ho. Mack was the hard-ass, yelling at them all like a drill sergeant. Dean was quietly bringing up the rear, helping them when things got really tough. In fact, he was carrying most of Luca and Adam's shit.

Adam was in the same boat as Luca, but he was being quiet about it all. He was definitely the closest to Charlie and had clearly been privy to harebrained plans of his in the past. But Luca could tell the dude wasn't happy about it.

They'd stopped for the night, and the guys were sitting around in a clearing, getting their beds ready and those gross MREs out for dinner.

Carb-coma was more like it.

"Where's Charlie?" Adam asked as he took off his boots. Luca wasn't taking shit off. If something came at him in the night, he wanted to be able to run.

"Went looking for wood." Luca checked his watch. Shit. "Fifteen minutes ago. I'll go check."

Standing, every muscle in his body protested. Who the hell needed to carry a thousand-pound log with four other guys on a daily basis? He was fucking over this shit.

He eased his way down the path Charlie had disappeared down, until he heard a groan. Then he picked up the pace.

Dammit.

Charlie was leaning against a tree, his ankle at an unnatural angle. It wasn't twisted. It was broken. His face was ashy gray, and he looked up at Luca with a pitiful look.

"Oops."

"Stay still. I got you." He turned and hollered, "Dean! Mack! He's wounded!" The trees and brush around him seemed to come alive as the rest of the guys came bumbling through it to get to them.

Dean took charge, which was unusual. Apparently, he had some experience with this shit.

"Mack, get me a splint. Adam and Luca, go back and start getting all the FRH's from the MREs. He's going into shock. And a fire. We'll need a fire." Dean went to work, ripping the bottom of his t-shirt, and Luca spun to go back to camp. He didn't want to see what happened next, although he could hear the crack of bone and Charlie's agonized cry.

The next hour was spent getting enough wood for a fire, while Adam gathered all the flameless heating things from the disgusting MREs. Luca didn't even want to know what sort of chemicals those gave off, but he was thankful for them, as they wrapped them in fabric and settled them around Charlie in various places. They were designed to heat food to edible temperature, not warm people, but whatever.

Two hours later, Charlie was settled next to the fire, covered with their blankets, still shivering. Luca had set out to actually cook a meal with what he'd brought along and a couple of rabbits that Dean had killed for them. He was going to make a soup. The broth would have protein for Charlie and the guys, and he'd brought a few herbs and seasonings to make it taste good.

"Dude, this is delicious." Adam slurped his hot broth.

They sat in silence, the danger of the situation sinking in for Luca.

"How will we get him out of here?"

Mack spoke up. "I'll build a travois for him. We'll take turns dragging. Me and Adam, you and Dean."

"Does anyone know how to get out?"

"Yeah. I do." Dean held up a piece of paper. "Charlie made a map. Dude thought of everything."

A wry chuckle escaped Luca. "When he said brotherhood, at first I thought he meant some sort of fight club. Like, we beat the shit out of each other. That's the only brotherhood I've known, that wasn't my actual brother." And there was plenty of shit beating there too. But when he'd first joined Forrester's gang, there had been an initiation that had almost put him in the hospital.

Adam spoke up. "His idea of brotherhood is different. He becomes brothers by saving. Not hurting." He was quiet when he said it and Luca knew they had a history, but had no clue what it was. Apparently it involved saving, because they were damn close.

Luca had his suspicions. This whole thing had been Charlie's idea from the get-go. He wanted to make them learn to work as a team before they started to take down Forrester. He'd said they needed to trust each other, learn to depend on each other, if they were going to be in this together.

Had the asshole broken his own ankle when he saw they were no more brothers than when they'd started this madness?

"How will we sleep? He's got all our blankets," Adam groused.

"Nuts to butts," Mack muttered.

"What?" Adam looked at him with alarm. Luca chuckled.

"We cuddle."

They didn't sleep much that night, wearing all the clothing they'd brought to stay warm in the freezing temperatures. But the next day, they managed to hump Charlie out of the wilderness and get him to safety.

And after all that teamwork, they were probably almost as close as brothers.

BONUS

Read on for an excerpt from the next book in the Dark Knights in the City series, Strange Love.

Luca has had his eye on the woman who eats at his restaurant with her friends each week. When his delivery driver is late, he fills in and discovers her drunk, lonely, and in dire need of a spanking.

Too bad Luca doesn't have time for romance. He's too busy working to take down the kingpin of the underworld, with his cronies, a group of like-minded guys. When they find out she's digging around in their business, they want her to disappear.

Heidi Jones wants romance with Luca, but she always picks the wrong guy. Based on the research she's doing on the city's changing crime patterns, this time, she picked the worst.

It's too late though. He's already got her and he's not letting go. He says he's protecting her, but she thinks it's something else.

CHAPTER ONE

Heidi loved the hustle and bustle of the newsroom around her. Listening to Bill do a phone interview with the assistant coach of the local baseball team, she knew she could have gotten an in-person interview. With the head coach. She always tried to do that. This guy was her main competition for the open news writer position, and Heidi had it in the bag. She'd been stuck in the women's section since she'd gotten the job, eight years ago, but she did all her interviews in person. It wasn't just reporting the person's words, but what they did, that told the story.

Even though Bill was the boss' nephew, Heidi knew she was more qualified for the job. Her interview had gone great. She'd been here longer, and she had better ideas.

"Hey, Heidi, you got that piece on the book boxes? I need eleven inches for page sixteen," Mr. Scroggins yelled across the room at her. Nobody looked up. He was always yelling at somebody.

"I sent it two weeks ago, but I'll shoot it to your inbox again. You need the pictures?" He waved absently, which she took as a yes. He never looked up from his laptop.

After sending the email, Heidi walked over to his desk, where he was buried in his computer screen, clicking away, his eyes magnified comically by his glasses. Stifling her smile, she stood in front of Mr. Scroggins.

"I sent the piece on Ms. Sharples' troop fundraiser."

He blinked at her, looking like she was speaking a foreign language.

"The boxes?" It took everything in her not to roll her eyes.

"No, sir, the Wounded Warrior fun run."

"Oh right. Right." He went back to his laptop, dismissing her.

"Sir? Did you get a chance to read over the story proposal I sent yesterday?"

He coughed. "The women's section doesn't do that sort of piece. We'll discuss it tomorrow after announcing the new news writer." He smiled at her brightly, and Heidi took a step back. It looked weird. She'd worked here for eight years and never noticed how many teeth the man had.

But he was going to talk about her proposed story idea after announcing the new position. She smiled gratefully at him, hoping to impart that she understood what he was saying.

"Meanwhile, the department heads need new desk chairs. Can you work something up for them to choose from?" Face hidden in his screen, she took that as her dismissal.

She wasn't even phased by the dismissal and sudden demotion to administrative assistant. It was temporary, unintentional, whatever. She would find them the best damn chairs for their buck, because she was sure she was getting the news writer position.

CHAPTER TWO

Bradley Cesnik was a man who didn't understand poker, much less the fact that the odds of the game will always be against him. That was why the douchebag was in Luca's office tossing out threats like a kid threatens the babysitter.

"I'll have you shut down." His attempt at menace came off as whining, and Luca simply smiled as Charlie came in the door behind him, his silver cane hiding the limp from his ankle he'd broken months ago in their "team building."

"Sit. We can discuss this." Magnanimously, Luca gestured to the chair by his desk. He was faking it, of course; he didn't have a single bone in his body that wished this guy well, but if Luca knew anything, it was that people underestimated the nice guy.

"There's nothing to discuss. Give me back my beach house, and I'll forget about it."

"That's not the way things work, and you know it. You signed the papers to get into the game you were so sure you'd win. But then, you didn't win, did you?" Luca settled himself into the other chair at his desk, folding his hands in front of him. Charlie stood in the back of the room, making Bradley visibly nervous. He didn't know who to look at, his body and head swiveling back and forth between the two men.

"I know people. All it will take is one word to the mayor."

Charlie laughed. "All it will take is one word to your wife."

"What do you mean?"

Luca took up the narrative as Charlie walked to the corner of the office where a baseball bat leaned, his cane thumping along the floor with his steps. "Does she know about that hot little piece you had on your arm that night? Does she even know you lost her family home? Doubt it. Just make up a story about the bank taking it or some shit, or she finds out about Chantel and her apartment in the city."

Chantel would probably be pissed if Luca fucked up her sugar daddy, but since Lady Jade's crew, a houseful of ladies of the night, were on Charlie's payroll, her current lodgings were just cream in her coffee anyway.

"What Luca is trying to say is you have a choice." Charlie leaned the cane against the wall and spun the bat in his hand. Even unbalanced, he wielded the bat like it was an extension of himself, and Luca was willing to bet he had a history with the sport. He knew just enough about Charlie to know he had likely never played organized sports anywhere, but for sure, he had always had a baseball bat with him. "You leave here quietly, nothing happens. You continue on this vein, and you'll be explaining an emergency room visit." Slamming the baseball bat into his hand, he gripped the wide end with his palm and reached behind him, under his coat. "Or, keep coming back, and you get a swift, painless end." Pulling out a 1911, he pointed it at Bradley's face. "So many options… Which will you choose?"

Bradley swallowed, weighing his options and clearly not liking any of the results.

"Fine. But you haven't heard the end of this." With one finger, he pushed the gun away as if it had cooties, and Luca smiled to himself. Bradley stood and exited the offices without a backward glance, his steps unsteady.

After the door slammed behind Bradley, Luca turned to Charlie, who was immaculately dressed as always in a dark suit. Reaching out, he grabbed his cane and leaned on it heavily. Charlie had broken his ankle in a trip they'd taken, one that Luca preferred to think of as a camping trip, not the hell it was. Either way, Charlie had healed marvelously, but was still a bit crippled. Sometimes, Luca thought he was using the cane for an affectation. Other times, like now, Luca wondered how badly he still needed it.

"I don't want him causing trouble. If he goes to the mayor, that's attention I don't want."

Charlie graced him with a rare smile. "Don't worry. How do you think the mayor got elected?"

"The incumbent he was running against died in a very public overdose episode."

Charlie spread his hands across the knob of his cane, leaning on it casually. "Accidents happen."

The dude creeped Luca out, but he was glad Charlie Delmonico was on his side. He didn't want enemies like that.

"Relax. This is temporary. A means to an end, and you know it. Just keep it up, and I'll take care of the troublemakers. Now, about tonight's shipment. Dean is ready with his team; do you anticipate trouble from your end of things?"

Luca's end of the deal consisted of keeping his ear to the ground with contacts he'd never wanted to have again. But his past had come back with a vengeance when these guys showed up in his bar, and retribution had dangled within his grasp. After discussing it with Nonna and his brother, he'd been on board, a little reluctantly, but now everything was in motion, with or without him.

"Yeah, Traylon says everything's going without a hitch, and he wants another payment before the next shipment to keep his trap shut."

"Understandable. I'll make it happen." Charlie straightened from where he'd been leaning on the wall. "I've got a meeting with Mack, and then another with Adam, and I'm picking up my girl from work to take her home. Luther will be there tonight, just in case, and I'll be on call."

"It's fine. I got it," Luca gritted out.

"I know."

He didn't want Luther breathing down his neck. He was creepier than Charlie, never talking to anyone but Charlie and Amelia. Luca got the impression he told them everything he saw, and he seemed to see a lot.

Charlie left the room with a soft click-step, his cane marking his stride.

HAVE YOU READ THESE?

Available Everywhere

https://melinda-owens.com/books/

Secrets We Keep

Ten years ago they brutally killed his wife while he was tied up, forced to watch, then they got off scot-free.

A decade he's been planning his revenge.

One phone call, and now everything's changed. They're after her twin sister, and Theo's the only one who can help her.

Perfect Drug

Charlie Delmonico is a fixer. It's what he does for a living. He fixes all the city's problems.

For a fee.

And he wants to fix Amelia's problems. Or use her for a fix, whichever works best.

Amelia works in the lobby of a building, until Charlie offers her a job she can't refuse. Does she want to be fixed, though? Or does she just want Charlie to see her? To know her?

When Charlie gets involved with a deal involving four other guys, to ruin the city's leader of the underworld, Amelia gets stuck in the middle.

She sees his true colors, and it tears them apart.

Even though Charlie is her perfect drug.

Strange Love

Luca has had his eye on the woman who eats at his restaurant with her friends each week. When his delivery driver is late, he fills in and discovers her drunk, lonely, and in dire need of a spanking.

Too bad Luca doesn't have time for romance. He's too busy working to take down the kingpin of the underworld, with his cronies, a group of like-minded guys. When they find out she's digging around in their business, they want her to disappear.

Heidi Jones wants romance with Luca, but she always picks the wrong guy. Based on the research she's doing on the city's changing crime patterns, this time, she picked the worst.

It's too late though. He's already got her and he's not letting go. He says he's protecting her, but she thinks it's something else.

Wicked Game

Mack has planned his part in the takedown of Bascom Forrester to the last detail, even the gorgeous IT director at the bank he's hacking into. He knows her past and is ready to use it against her.

But he doesn't anticipate her fire. Her loyalty to her job. Her utter hatred of him. And he finds that he loves every bit of that.

Greer has spent her adult life overcoming her past and dealing with it. Along comes Mack, who undermines her at every turn. When she finds she can't get away, she tries to lull him into complacency, but that backfires in a big way.

She can't seem to extricate herself from the web he's drawn around her, and the more she discovers of his motivations, the less she wants to.

Come Undone

Dean's wife was murdered, while leaving him to be with Forrester. Forrester decided it would be less hassle to kill her than keep a mistress. Dean has blamed the other man for ruining his life ever since, so when he finds the rest of the guys trying to wreak vengeance on Forrester, he's all in. Unfortunately, his talents are few and far between. He's good for brute force, and that's about it.

Emma is a bank teller, in the unfortunate position of catching Dean's eye during his first robbery. As she's taken hostage and stripped of all control, she ends up finding something she didn't realize she'd lost.

Sometimes, to be put back together, you must first come undone.

Bittersweet Symphony

Adam Beckett has a secret, and the only one who knows it is Jennifer Forrester. Of course, she doesn't remember, which makes his revenge that much sweeter.

Jennifer can't figure out exactly what Adam needs from her, but he's willing to marry her to give her foster son a home.

As usual, she's caught up in something she doesn't understand. As she gains clarity and remembers what it is Adam needs her to understand, she realizes she playing one instrument in a symphony.

While she is finding herself and a hidden strength she'd never been allowed to explore, her father is driving her away from Adam.

And she's not sure he can come back from it.

ABOUT MELINDA

Melinda Owens was born in 2020, when the world turned dark. Her previous muses leaving her, she recreated herself as a darker author, saving her own sanity in a world with happily-ever-afters in spite of her own frustrating circumstances. She lives in East Texas with an abundance of cats and her family of giant people.

Contact Melinda

Sign up for the newsletter: https://wp.me/Pda8v3-T

Website: www.melinda-owens.com

Facebook: https://www.facebook.com/melindaowensauthor

MO's Place (reader group) https://www.facebook.com/groups/662888238425819

Tiktok: http://tiktok.com/@author.meldina.owens?

Email: melindaowensauthor@gmail.com

CPSIA information can be obtained
at www.ICGtesting.com
Printed in the USA
LVHW021404060522
717863LV00014B/702

9 781950 264247